"*She* has already been called and is on the way..."

Daniel knew precisely who *she* was without his deputy needing to say it.

Chief of police Wilhelmina "Willa" Nelson. As much as Sheriff Daniel Clark enjoyed the sight of her, as well as her company once upon a time before they'd both held their respective positions, he was not looking forward to their next conversation.

Coming up the hill, Willa emerged—a striking brunette in jeans and a white button-down with her badge displayed on her hip.

He focused his attention on the formidable woman making her way to him like a heat-seeking missile. Tall and slender, Willa was all sinewy muscle with the perfect balance of curves. She radiated strength. Not only in her trim build, but also from her sharp mind and her unyielding spirit.

Beneath her cowboy hat, long, dark hair fell to her shoulders in loose waves, framing a compelling face that he took far too much pleasure staring at. Willa aimed a steely glance his way as she slowed her ground-eating stride. "Sheriff Clark."

Daniel gritted his teeth at the cool formality between them that had replaced the warmth of familiarity. "Chief Nelson," he said, tipping his Stetson at her.

WYOMING MOUNTAIN COLD CASE

Juno Rushdan

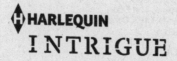

HARLEQUIN
INTRIGUE

For Gloria—my aunt, my second mother, my best friend.

HARLEQUIN®
INTRIGUE™

ISBN-13: 978-1-335-59045-9

Wyoming Mountain Cold Case

Copyright © 2023 by Juno Rushdan

Recycling programs
for this product may
not exist in your area.

For questions and comments about the quality of this book,
please contact us at CustomerService@Harlequin.com.

Harlequin Enterprises ULC
22 Adelaide St. West, 41st Floor
Toronto, Ontario M5H 4E3, Canada
www.Harlequin.com

Printed in U.S.A.

Juno Rushdan is a veteran US Air Force intelligence officer and award-winning author. Her books are action-packed and fast-paced. Critics from *Kirkus Reviews* and *Library Journal* have called her work "heart-pounding James Bond-ian adventure" that "will captivate lovers of romantic thrillers." For a free book, visit her website: www.junorushdan.com.

Books by Juno Rushdan

Harlequin Intrigue

Cowboy State Lawmen

Wyoming Winter Rescue
Wyoming Christmas Stalker
Wyoming Mountain Hostage
Wyoming Mountain Murder
Wyoming Cowboy Undercover
Wyoming Mountain Cold Case

Fugitive Heroes: Topaz Unit

Rogue Christmas Operation
Alaskan Christmas Escape
Disavowed in Wyoming
An Operative's Last Stand

A Hard Core Justice Thriller

Hostile Pursuit
Witness Security Breach
High-Priority Asset
Innocent Hostage
Unsuspecting Target

Tracing a Kidnapper

Visit the Author Profile page at Harlequin.com.

CAST OF CHARACTERS

Daniel Clark—This cowboy sheriff is thrown into a dangerous murder investigation where he must work with the chief of police to find a killer before it's too late.

Wilhelmina "Willa" Nelson—As the new chief of police, she would prefer to have full jurisdiction over the case. But when the handsome sheriff gets too close, she can't let him find out that it's not only her job she's trying to protect.

Zeke Nelson—Willa's troubled son.

Grace Clark—Daniel's sister and Holden's fiancée.

Holden Powell—Chief deputy and soon to be Daniel's brother-in-law.

Marshall McCoy—The charismatic leader of the Shining Light. He will do anything to safeguard his compound, his people and his secrets.

Prologue

November. Five years ago.

I'm going to die!

On this freezing mountain, he's going to kill me.

No, no, don't give up. Don't let him win. You have to fight!

But how?

Tiffany Cummings tugged at the thick ropes that dug into her wrists, trembling from the fierce sting of icy wind on her bare flesh. She was on the frozen ground, bound with each arm tied to a tree. Her ankles were tied tight together. Unable to even scratch at the rope, she had no idea how she could possibly get free, much less fight.

A gust of wind howled through the snow-capped, forsaken mountain ridges surrounding her. She might have a chance...if only she was alone.

But she wasn't.

The madman who had lured her in and kidnapped her was close. She couldn't see him now, but she felt his dark presence as surely as the bite of the wind.

He was getting ready to take her life.

Why had she been foolish enough to trust him, to accept his help? What had it been about him that caused her to lower her guard?

Had it been his concern for her? His charming smile? His handsome face? His kind words of assurance? Those intelligent green eyes? That it was the holidays, the day after Thanksgiving in her small, peaceful town that had always been safe?

Regardless of the reason, when she'd gotten the flat tires, she'd trusted him and had been deceived. He'd chased her through the mountain. No…hunted her. Like a predator stalking his prey. Knocked her unconscious. And when she came to, opening her eyes, she was trapped in her worst nightmare.

Stripped down to her underwear. Shivering. Bound. Gagged with duct tape over her lips. Barely able to breathe. Waiting for him to kill her while her body grew numb from the cold and the fear.

Snow crunched beneath his feet, footfalls drawing nearer.

Her heart raced. She yanked on the ropes again. Pain cut through her shoulder. Bitter cold from the hard, frozen ground seeped deeper into her bones and she set her jaw against it.

His breath crystallized in the air above her near the trunk of the sturdy pine as he stepped into view. A vicious wolf in sheep's clothing.

He'd even howled like a wolf, baying at the moon when he'd started hunting her.

Now his green eyes found hers, pinning her with his cruel gaze. She kicked out at him, but it was no use. He stayed well out of the range of her feet.

Something glinted in his hand. Metal winked in the moonlight.

A knife. Big and long. Razor-sharp. The kind used for butchering and gutting game.

Her stomach clenched. Hot bile flooded her throat.

Why? She blinked back tears, but the warm drops fell nonetheless, freezing on her cheeks. *Oh God, why me?*

His mouth was covered by a ski mask, but she could tell he was smiling from the way his eyes lit up like it was Christmas. And she was the gift he was about to rip into.

No, no, no!

She couldn't let him get away with this. He

had to be stopped. Punished. She'd fought him earlier and scratched his skin. The police would trace his DNA under her fingernails. They'd find him and catch him.

They had to.

But how long before her body was found? Nobody would notice her absence or report her missing. No one might stumble upon her until the next hunting season started.

He lowered to the ground, kneeling beside her.

Panic surged through her blood, making her heart thunder.

"No!" Tiffany tried to scream, but the duct tape muffled her cries. She tried to break free of her restraints, but the ropes were too thick, too tightly fastened. If she were able, she'd beg for her life, offer to do anything if only he'd spare her.

Dear God, help me.

Looming over her, he stared down at her face. Those icy green eyes gleamed in the moonlight. He peeled the tape from her mouth.

A million different things whirled in her mind, but she could only muster one word. "Why?"

"Because I can."

Tiffany whimpered. There was nothing she

could say or do to stop him. Nothing at all. "Why me?"

"Someone had to be the first and you made it so easy. So much fun toying with you."

A sob bubbled up her throat, but he pressed the tape back over her lips before her cries left her mouth.

"You won't be alone," he said. "There'll be others." He raised the knife.

Tiffany squeezed her eyes shut, knowing… she was as good as dead.

Chapter One

In the waning light of day, Sheriff Daniel Clark crouched down beside the dead woman. The cool October wind kicked up and the tang of fresh blood hit him, the smell like wet pennies mixed with musty earth.

He'd been in law enforcement for a long time. Eighteen years, most of which had been at the Southeastern Wyoming University's police department. He'd experienced the gamut over nearly two decades, but in this part of the country crime was low and things stayed relatively uneventful the majority of the time. Until he'd taken over as sheriff and the floodgates from hell opened. In the past twenty-four months, there'd been one thing after another: domestic violence, murder, rape, arson, drug cartel activity, a hostage crisis, even domestic terrorists shooting up the town in an attempt to kill a federal agent.

The depths to which humanity could sink

no longer shocked him, though it always sickened him. But this was different. He'd never seen anything quite like it.

The woman had been stripped to her undergarments, her arms extended and wrists bound to the base of tree trunks with rope. Ghostly white skin that was turning blue. Her throat had been viciously slashed. Multiple uneven bloody gashes in her chest.

Whoever this woman was, she had once been beautiful. Angular face. Slender body. Her brown eyes were wide and still with that startled expression death tended to leave them in. Long, dark hair was fanned out around her head, as though it had been carefully positioned that way by her killer, like a crown.

The person who took her life had taken the time to make a spectacle of her death.

Daniel looked around past the flash of yellow crime scene tape, ignoring one of his deputies who was embroiled in a dispute over jurisdiction with a police officer. He took in the isolated surroundings of the woods, where the woman had been stumbled upon by two campers.

Why here? In this heavily wooded area with minimal foot traffic if the killer had planned to go through the effort of putting her on display.

He glanced at the neatly folded pile of women's clothing off to the side, and then over his shoulder. "Officer? You didn't touch the clothes, did you?"

"No way, Sheriff," said the LPD patrol officer. "Left the body and clothes in situ," he said.

Good. If they were lucky, they might find a wallet or ID in a pocket. He didn't dare disturb anything until forensics took pictures of the entire scene.

As the heels of his boots sank into the grass, he looked back down at the victim. From the deep ligature marks, it appeared she had struggled while tied up before she died.

Jane Doe was a fighter.

But there weren't any defensive wounds or other bruises on her face or body. Yet, the perpetrator had managed to undress her without any apparent injury to her. Had she been drugged?

Peering closer at her wrist, he noticed a tattoo. A crescent moon next to a sun with an eye at the center. The symbol of the Shining Light cult.

For a few breaths, he stayed crouched, marking the woman's passing. The loss of a daughter, possibly a sister, someone's friend.

"Deputy Russo." Daniel beckoned to her as he stood.

Ashley, a sturdy redhead with long hair that

she wore in a single braid, approached him with frustration stamped across her flush face. "LPD is going to make a stink about this. *She* has already been called and is on the way."

Daniel knew precisely who *she* was without his deputy needing to say it.

Chief of police Wilhelmina "Willa" Nelson. As much as he enjoyed the sight of her, as well as her company once upon a time before they'd both held their respective positions, he was not looking forward to their next conversation.

"You measured it?" Daniel asked.

Ashley gave a curt nod. "Just like you requested. Measured it twice to be sure. That tree line there marks the end of Laramie city limits. Fifteen feet from the body. This one is ours."

It was a good thing Ashley was meticulous. He could count on her accuracy, which he was going to need in the next few minutes.

"Okay." He stifled a groan. Willa would fight it. Almost everything between them had become a point of contention. "The victim has a tattoo of the Shining Light." He turned toward the expanse of woods. "Any idea how far their compound is from here?"

"Not exactly. Rough guess would be two, maybe three miles that way." She pointed in the direction he was already facing.

Daniel had limited interaction with the leader of the cult, Marshall McCoy. The man was as charismatic as he was evasive. McCoy had a reputation throughout law enforcement circles for cooperating only when it suited his own interests and a knack for stonewalling when it didn't.

"Forensics is here," Ashley said.

Coming up the hill was their crime scene investigator, Deputy Nina Pruitt. A new hire and transfer from Cheyenne as a result of the increase in budget he'd finally gotten approved. Up until then, they hadn't had a trained forensic scientist in the department. His small team had to collect the evidence themselves and send it to a third party to be processed.

A few feet behind Deputy Pruitt, Willa emerged—a striking brunette in jeans and a white button-down with her badge displayed on her hip.

"Give Nina a hand while I handle this," Daniel said, removing his nitrile gloves as he slipped under the yellow tape cordoning off the area.

"Better you than me." Ashley gave him a wary look. "Good luck." She greeted the other deputy.

Daniel nodded hello to Pruitt. She was young, but seasoned and smart. They were fortunate to have gotten her when she had other opportunities. Some might say bigger and better ones with more room for advancement.

He refocused his attention on the formidable woman making her way to him like a heat-seeking missile. Tall and slender, Willa was all sinewy muscle with the perfect balance of curves. She radiated strength. Not only in her trim build. More so from her sharp mind and her unyielding spirit.

Beneath her cowboy hat, long, dark hair fell to her shoulders in loose waves, framing a compelling face that he took far too much pleasure staring at. Willa aimed a steely glance his way as she slowed her ground-eating stride. "Sheriff Clark."

Daniel gritted his teeth at the cool formality between them that had replaced the warmth of familiarity. "Chief Nelson," he said, tipping his Stetson at her.

He wanted to believe that if they had been alone, which they never were these days, rather than in the presence of subordinates, things might have been closer to their former normal. No posturing. No titles. Only the sweet ease and sultry heat they'd once shared.

"According to my officer," she said, "the body was left in the same manner as my current case."

"From what I read in the paper, it was." He wouldn't have to speculate on the similarities of the crimes if she had loaded the case in ViCAP, the Violent Crime Apprehension Program database that allowed investigators to compare incident details with thousands of other crimes. But that would have assumed Willa had the time to do so. He was aware time was something she was short on with the current constraints of the LPD. "I'm not sure what information you withheld from reporters. There was no mention of any identifying marks on the body. Did yours happen to have a tattoo?"

Willa nodded. "Shining Light symbol. On her shoulder. I take it this one is the same."

"It is. But the tattoo is on her wrist."

She folded her arms. With those razor-edge cheekbones and rigid stance she looked ready for tug-of-war. "Then I think we can both agree the murders are linked. Since I'm already neck-deep in an open investigation it only makes sense that this case is also mine."

"Not so fast. This body is beyond town limits."

"I'll need to verify that and even if it is, by how much?" she asked, her brown doe eyes narrowing. "One foot, two? We're talking mere inches. No need to muddy the waters on this one."

"Fifteen feet. Which makes this victim unquestionably beyond your authority. Makes it *mine*." He took a deep breath. "We're on the same side and have the same goal. To catch a killer. I don't want to fight with you."

"Then don't." She placed her hands on the snug denim over her hips, the small movement dragging his mind to a moment when they'd both been free from the responsibility of their current positions, skin to skin, the heady taste of her on his tongue.

The memory made his chest ache. He wasn't quite sure why. Their fling, if it could even be called that, had been sudden, intense, scorching, like a flash fire. Not meant to last.

"If only it was that simple," he said.

"It is. Step aside and stay out of my way."

The harder they tried to stay out of each other's orbit, the more circumstances beyond their control yanked them back together. First, his department was located in her town out of all the others in the county. There was no way to avoid one another. Just last month the domestic terrorists gunning for a federal agent had left them no choice but to join forces to save countless lives and protect the town.

Now a serial killer was driving them together once again. Collaboration was inevitable, whether she liked it or not.

DANIEL STRUCK HER as a good guy, not the kind to manipulate her with the power of his position, but she'd been fooled before by the wrong man. It had nearly cost her her life.

Why couldn't he make this easy for both of them and simply agree to let her handle this case?

For some reason, he wasn't going to. It was written all over his handsome face, so handsome it should've been illegal. She saw it in the hard set of his jaw, in the stiff defiance of his six feet two inches of lean muscle. All of which only irritated her more than his obstinance.

"Afraid I can't do that," he said in that smooth, easy tone of his that would brook no argument.

The smell of cinnamon gum and cedar drifted over her, an enticing mix she'd come to associate with Daniel. "Why not?"

"The killer placed the victim here. Outside of your jurisdiction. Nothing I can do to change that. Also, you have to consider the perp might not be finished. Another body could turn up. The next one could be even farther from the town limit."

A distinct possibility that spiked her irritation even higher. It was one she'd rather not entertain, but it was unavoidable. "What do you propose?" she asked, rolling back her shoulders, steeling herself for his response.

If he insisted on taking over the case and cutting her out, which he could do as the highest law enforcement officer of the county, then she'd fight it tooth and nail. Not that she'd have much recourse. Even so, she wasn't going to simply hand him her case. With as many supporters as she had critics, every day she had to prove herself. This might be the twenty-first century, but it was still a male-dominated field, where many still didn't trust her to do the job on the sole basis of her gender.

Everything she had she'd either earned or fought for, and this case was no different.

"Our departments should work together on this," he said.

Surprise had her struggling not to flinch at the idea. She stared in his eyes, cool, brown and unfathomable. "Working with one of your deputies is acceptable. My preference would be Holden Powell."

She knew enough about Powell to believe they wouldn't have a problem getting along. He'd been injured in the shootout with the domestic terrorists, but he was on the mend and back in the office.

"Holden returning to work so soon after being shot didn't sit well with my sister. He's on vacation."

"Let me guess, they're dating."

"Actually, they're engaged and living together. It happened rather quickly. Too quickly."

Not even three degrees of separation in this town. "Well, then, assign someone else."

A smile curved his lips. "I was thinking you and me on this one."

Willa scoffed. There were several good reasons for that not to happen. Top among them being distraction. This job required her full focus. The pressure was immense. There wasn't room for diversions. Or complications. "I'd prefer to keep this investigation clean. No muddy waters."

She'd taken great pains to ensure her personal life didn't bleed over into her professional one. Particularly since when it did, it tended to hemorrhage.

Once she started as chief of the LPD around the same time Daniel donned the badge as sheriff, she'd ended things between them. Before their hearts got entangled and it became something serious that was destined to end badly, as things invariably did for her.

An ounce of prevention was worth a pound of cure.

"Look, the LPD is overwhelmed right now," he said. "You've lost most of your detectives and you're running a barebones department. Any assistance, even if it's from me, should be viewed as helpful."

All true, not that he needed to rub her face in the fact. The mayor had hired her not only because she was qualified but also because she was from Wayward Bluffs and not Laramie. There had been suspicion of dirty cops in the LPD. She was brought in to clean it up and she had. Though the fallout was greater than anyone had expected, leaving a serious personnel shortage and her working double duty putting in eighteen-hour days.

Daniel eyed her, probably trying to figure out her reluctance. "If you're worried about which department will get the credit—"

"It's not that." The only thing that mattered was catching a killer. "I don't want lines to blur," Willa said, hoping he'd understand her concerns without the need to say more with others in earshot.

Unfortunately, some people, a few of them cops, had the gall to imply she'd slept her way to the top. The last thing she wanted was for her brief dalliance with Daniel two years ago to become known and end up as fodder for the local gossips.

"Two women have lost their lives," he said. "I think we can keep it professional. Clean slate?" He proffered his hand.

As much as she wanted to, she couldn't dismiss the sincerity in his eyes. "All right." She shook his hand. His palm was incredibly warm, the heat enticing her to relax. She ended the contact before he did, but his touch left her fingers tingling.

Willa looked away at the crime scene. The evidence tech had finished examining the body. She treaded around carefully, photographing the area, circling the grim landscape, documenting every angle and piece of whatever had been left behind.

"Where exactly did you find the last body?" Daniel asked.

"Not far from here." She pointed east, closer to town. "Less than a quarter a mile."

"What did Marshall McCoy have to say about the first victim when you questioned him?"

She frowned. "I spoke with a public relations representative. McCoy was *indisposed*." All acolytes forsook their worldly possessions and took the new surname Starlight, sometimes changing their forenames as well after their vows. Willa didn't get the appeal of the cult. Apparently, many others did. There were more than five hundred people living on the compound. "They claim the victim, Blue Starlight, formerly Beverly Fisher, was no longer a part of their community and was considered to be one of the Fallen."

"The Fallen?"

"That's what they call someone who has left or been kicked out and is no longer welcomed to return."

Daniel quirked a brow. "Did they say why she left?"

"Not really. Only that she decided the commune was no longer for her about four months ago. That's it. Fisher ended up homeless."

"Do you buy it? Why would she give up shelter, safety and hot meals to live on the streets?"

Willa shrugged. "McCoy and his front person for the Shining Light clearly have an agenda. The preservation of their pristine reputation. They won't say anything that'll reflect poorly. Fisher leaving four months ago checked out. No one in town she associated with afterward knew why she'd left. There's definitely more to the story, but the cultists aren't talking."

"With two murdered women from his commune, McCoy will have no choice but to talk."

"Sure, he'll talk. His mouth will open, words will spill out, but he won't say anything pertinent." The man had dodge-and-evade down to a science. "Let's wait until we know more, time of death and hopefully a name of the victim, before we go knocking on his gate." She meant that metaphorically since the last time she was at the compound they'd requested she make an appointment if there were any additional questions. "Ideally, I'd like to talk to someone who knew her outside of the compound first. It'd be nice to have something to go on when we question McCoy."

"All right. That'll give me a chance to look at your case file. I can input the details into ViCAP."

Loading the case in the database would have made coordination with the sheriff's department easier if she'd already done it. "I've barely had time to eat, much less sleep, with none to spare on ViCAP." Nonetheless it was a valuable tool. One she should've made time for sooner. "Sorry about that."

"I wasn't criticizing. You've got your hands full. I never did get a chance to tell you how impressive it was the way you cleaned house, getting rid of all those dirty cops. Couldn't have been easy."

"Took patience and persistence. A lot of

sleepless nights devising a way to catch them without any of them seeing it coming." All those police officers had been cunning enough to get away with corruption for years. Nailing them had been the most difficult undertaking of her life. "Bringing in the state attorney general's office was the key. I wouldn't have managed it without one of their undercover agents from DCI," she said referring to the Division of Criminal Investigation.

"You'll accept help from the DCI with no problem, but not me?"

"I don't like to be beholden. Especially not to someone who lives in my backyard."

"Well on this, we'll be helping each other."

"Yeah, sure," she said, her voice clipped, her mouth dry. In the end, she hoped that was how it worked out. "I'll make sure you get the file."

"Sheriff!" Deputy Pruitt called. "There's an ID in her pocket."

Willa and Daniel headed back to the cordoned-off area.

"With Fisher, did you find a wallet or identification in her clothes?" he asked Willa.

"Nope. If only we'd been so lucky," she said. "They had to ID her for us at the compound."

"What do we have?" Daniel asked as they approached the boundary of the yellow tape.

"Her name was Leslie Gooding. Student ID card. SWU."

Convenient that Daniel had been the chief of campus police. "Do you know any school officials willing to come in after hours to access student records?" Willa asked him.

"I stay in contact with a couple of administrators. At least one of them might be able to help out tonight. Worst case, first thing in the morning, but I should give my replacement on campus a heads-up about this."

An unnecessary courtesy since the body wasn't discovered on school property. It spoke volumes about Daniel as a professional and as a person.

"While you're doing that, I'll formulate a statement for the press. Similar to what I put out about Fisher." It was better to feed the reporters her narrative before they caught wind of another murder and painted their own picture.

"I think we should give them more details this time. Mention the tattoo of the Shining Light."

"Are you sure that's a good idea?"

He didn't look certain. "It'll put public pressure on McCoy to cooperate more fully if nothing else."

It could also backfire in a number of ways.

"We'll see how it plays out." Willa glanced back at the tech. "Any estimate on the time of death?"

"Based on the body temp and conditions, I'd say it's somewhere between midnight and five a.m. Once I take her in, the medical examiner will be able to give a more precise time. The stab wounds to her chest are deep. Jagged edges to the cuts. You're looking for a serrated knife. Like one used for hunting. Fairly big."

"The same as with Fisher," Willa said. "We didn't find one at the scene." Her cell phone buzzed. She pulled it from her back pocket and glanced at the screen. Wayward Bluffs police department. She groaned at the inkling of why her former department would be calling. "Excuse me. I've got to take this," she said. Turning, she stepped away and answered, "This is Nelson."

"Hello, Chief. This is Cannedy."

"What's up?"

"Bad news." The somber tone of his voice struck her.

"Spit it out, Cannedy. You know I hate suspense."

"Sorry to bother you, but it's about Zeke."

Her heart nearly dropped out of her chest. "Ezekiel?" With suddenly trembling hands, she started down the hill toward her SUV. She checked for any lurking reporters as she hurried but didn't see any. "What happened? Was there a car accident?" Her son had a reckless streak. He always drove faster than he should, taking tricky turns at a high speed. Blood-curdling images flashed in her mind. First, of his body trapped in a mass of twisted metal and then him in a hospital on life support.

What would she do if she lost him?

"No, ma'am, nothing like that. He's okay." Cannedy took a breath, but Willa couldn't shake the fear of a senseless tragedy snuffing out the life of her only child. "He's been arrested."

In an instant, her panic slid to anger. "Arrested?" That boy was going to be the death of her. "What has my son done this time?"

Chapter Two

As Daniel finished inputting the details of the Fisher case into the national database, his thoughts careened back to Willa. She'd taken off from the crime scene in such a hurry. Only an emergency or a herd of wild horses could have dragged her away. He hoped everything was all right.

He'd known her two and a half years, but he didn't *know her* in that way. Only the first six months counted toward the getting better acquainted part until she'd ghosted him. He'd spent some time with her, enough to get a bead on her personality, read her mood. Even then, she'd been too guarded to let him in. He didn't know a thing about her past, or about her life. Other than the fact she was single and had spent almost half her life as a cop in Wayward Bluffs.

That hadn't stopped him from asking her if everything was okay after her phone call tonight. Her tightlipped response, which had told him absolutely nothing, had been expected.

A knock on his door pulled his gaze from the computer up to his injured chief deputy and future brother-in-law.

"What are you doing here?" Daniel asked. "Are you trying to get me into trouble with my sister?" Their relationship was strained enough. Daniel didn't need to do anything to make it worse.

Holden chuckled as though Daniel had been joking. With an arm in a sling, his chief deputy leaned against the doorjamb. "Grace and I are running errands in town. While she's at the hospital discussing changes to her schedule with her supervisor, I thought I'd swing by, see what was going on and invite you to a big family dinner out at the ranch tomorrow night."

Swallowing a sigh, Daniel lowered his head.

"Before you say no, for the third time," Holden said, "not coming won't make the invitations stop. It'll only add fuel to my mother's fire to break bread with you and discuss the wedding."

"Pick a date for the ceremony, tell me what to wear and I'll be there on time. You don't need me for wedding planning."

"I don't. But Grace does. Which means Holly Powell has made it her mission to include you every step of the way. Once my mama gets fixed on something, nothing can stop her. Just ask my dad."

Daniel wasn't buying it that Grace wanted him there. When she'd relocated from California to get away from their overbearing mother, he'd offered her a room at his place—a rundown ranch their father had bequeathed him, where he kept two horses. With his full-time job as sheriff, he'd imagined getting a couple more mares with her help. Showing her what their dad had loved about the Cowboy State, the land, the great outdoors—this place. But his younger sister had turned him down flat, opting to rent an even more ramshackle cabin instead of staying with family and saving money.

Now she was living with Holden. Blissfully fitting in among the Powell clan out on the six thousand gasp-inducing acres of a working ranch, the Shooting Star.

He wanted her to be happy, to find a place where she belonged. What decent brother would begrudge her that?

It was nice she was here, nearby. If only her proximity had brought them closer.

With a twelve-year age gap and their father dying before she was born, they had never had a typical sibling relationship. He'd moved out by the time she was six. During his visits while she was growing up, he'd done his best to fill in the holes of whatever was missing in her life, but he never seemed to get it right.

"Are you sure your mom isn't the one pushing for me to come?" Daniel asked. "For the sake of appearances." He'd play whatever part they wanted for the ceremony, but he didn't want to go where he wasn't truly welcomed. "My sister isn't the one here asking." And invites to dinner didn't start coming until there was chitchat of a wedding.

"She doesn't know I came here to talk about this." Holden crossed the threshold, stepping into the office. "I think she's uncertain where you stand on our relationship. I am, too, to be honest. It's not as if you've given us your blessing."

Daniel leaned back in his chair, the words hitting him like a sucker punch. "I didn't think she needed it." Or cared about it for that matter. "You're two consenting adults and I congratulated you both."

With a half-hearted nod, Holden said, "Sort of. There didn't seem to be any joy behind the words. It was…awkward."

Their relationship, much less their engagement, had been a shock to Daniel. At the time, his deputy had merely been a colleague looking out for Daniel's little sister. Grace was safe and although she was single, she'd never even indicated she liked Holden. "I went out of town for two weeks. Ten days to be precise. And I get back to find out Grace was nearly killed and suddenly living with you." Talk about awkward. "Then you two are engaged after only a couple of months." Six weeks to be exact. "It was all rather fast. Unexpected. I didn't mean to give the impression that I didn't approve." Though he didn't see the reason to rush down to the altar either. "Even if you didn't ask my permission or for her hand in marriage."

He might only be her brother, but he was also the only father figure she'd ever known. Nonetheless, his opinion didn't matter when they started their relationship. It certainly wasn't a factor regarding their engagement. Why was he supposed to think his blessing—or lack thereof—would concern either of them?

"Is that the problem?" Holden asked.

Not wanting to go down that road, Daniel stood. "There is no problem. Honestly, you're great for my sister. I've never seen her so happy and at ease." She even transitioned from working palliative care that had been draining her emotionally to getting her master's degree in nursing administration. "I'm glad you two connected. I only wish it had happened under better circumstances. Okay?"

"Then you'll come to dinner?"

"You just don't give up."

Holden shrugged. "It's a part of my charm. I guess I get it from my mom."

Ready to inform Holden that his charm was a figment of his imagination, another knock on the door saved him.

"Sheriff, am I interrupting?" Pruitt asked.

"No, you're not." *Right on time.* "Come on in." Daniel waved her inside the room when she hesitated.

"The medical examiner will start the autopsy at eight a.m.," Pruitt said.

"There's a second body?" Holden asked.

"Yeah," Daniel said with a slight nod. "This one is ours. She's been identified. One of my contact's at SWU, where the victim was a student, gave me her parents' contact information in Cheyenne. The local PD will notify them tonight. But Chief Nelson and I will be working the case together."

Holden's brows rose in surprise. "Chief Nelson? I'm shocked she agreed."

Not that Daniel had given her much choice.

"Do you want me to take a look at the case?" Holden asked, gesturing to the file Pruitt held in her hand.

"That's all right. Grace will be waiting. I don't want to keep you." Daniel took the file from Pruitt and set it on his desk. "Let her know that with these murders, I'll have some late nights ahead. Dinner will have to wait."

Holden's mouth flattened into a grim line. "She won't like it, but she'll understand. My mama on the other hand is a different story."

The perfect way to handle Holly Powell was with two words. Selene Beauvais. "The person who should really be involved in all this is our mother."

Holden grimaced. "No disrespect, but I think her participation in the planning might stress out Grace. We want to keep things simple."

There was no doubt about it. Selene Beauvais was stress personified. For everyone. But she was still their mother.

"There's no way I can tell my mom I'm included in wedding planning while she isn't." Daniel threw his hands up. "It might be best for the mothers of the groom and the bride to Skype, FaceTime, something." Let Holly deal with it, sparing both Grace and him. "Before my mother decides to hop on a plane and invite herself to dinner, which is entirely possible if she feels excluded." Then Daniel would have to clean up the mess that would be left in the wake of Hurricane Selene. He stepped around the desk, putting a hand on Holden's shoulder, and steered him to the door. "Tell my sister I can always make time to have a cup of coffee with her."

"Understood." Holden took the hint and left.

"Do you need anything else tonight?" Pruitt asked.

He'd nearly forgotten she was still standing there, silent as a fly on the wall. "No. It's getting late. You should head home." The phone on his desk rang.

"I'll be in early tomorrow," Pruitt said. "Have a good night."

"Night." He picked up the phone. "Albany County Sheriff's Department. Sheriff Clark speaking."

"This is Detective Johnson of Cheyenne PD. We notified Mr. and Mrs. Gooding about the death of their daughter. I'll email you a copy of their statement, but they intend to drive down to Laramie tomorrow morning to speak with you. They also want to see their daughter's body."

Daniel couldn't imagine what those poor people must be going through, the magnitude of grief. "It'll be good to speak with them first-hand. Do they know an autopsy will have to be performed before they can see her?"

"I told them. But they insisted. You should expect them first thing in the morning."

"All right. Thank you, Detective."

Hanging up, he sat at his desk and opened the file. It was a digital world, but he was old-school and it helped him to have everything in black-and-white in his hands. Staring at the photos of Leslie Gooding, his heart sank, but a fire to find her killer ignited in his veins.

Daniel took out his cell and texted Willa.

DOING HER BEST to keep shame from surfacing on her face, Willa followed Cannedy back to the holding cells. Her cell phone in her hand chimed. She read the text.

Tomorrow a.m. Gooding's parents are coming from Cheyenne. My office.

Too distracted to be annoyed the interview would take place at his office rather than hers, Willa sent a quick reply.

Sure. Be there at 9. Let me know if they show sooner.

She doubted that they would. It was a forty-five-minute drive from Cheyenne. The Goodings probably wouldn't get much sleep tonight, but she didn't expect them to knock on the sheriff's door at the crack of dawn. Her phone chimed.

Ok. Autopsy will begin at 8. Hope all is well with you.

Everything was not well. It was a mess, but it could've been worse. At least Zeke was alive. She could still wrap her arms around her son and hold him tight. If he'd let her.

Instead of responding to the text, she slipped her phone in her pocket. Oddly enough, the timing of having assistance on this case was working out in her favor. With Daniel handling things at the moment, she could focus on her son, who needed her full attention.

"I really appreciate the phone call, Sergeant," she said. On the outside, she was unflappable. On the inside, her chest was deflating like a tire with a slow leak.

"The new chief says this is the last favor," Cannedy said, keys jangling in his hands. "Two strikes so far. Next time we have to bring Zeke in and—"

"I understand." Her son would be treated like anybody else. Booked, charged and forced to face the consequences of his actions. "Thanks again for calling me."

"Think nothing of it. Least I could do." At the cell, Cannedy unlocked the door. "You're free to go."

Pushing his long hair back with his fingers, Zeke lifted his head, his gaze meeting hers. "Uh-huh," he said, as his way of greeting, and she stiffened. Hopping up from the bench, her twenty-one-year-old problem child smirked. "Color me surprised."

His ingratitude made her blood boil. "Not another word from you until we're outside."

He snapped his heels together and gave her a mock salute.

Cannedy, his eyebrows two thick slashes of disgust that matched his flattened lips, let go of the opened cell door. "I'll leave you to it, ma'am."

Once the sergeant was out of the holding area, she said, "Come on, and don't do anything to embarrass me further on the way out."

Zeke trudged out of the cell past her, reeking of alcohol.

Thank God he was alive. Unhurt. That was her one consolation.

They walked down the corridor in silence and through the bullpen. Most of the officers in tonight avoided eye contact. Those who didn't stared at her with either pity or disdain. She hated being the subject of either.

Throwing a hand up in farewell to Cannedy, she shoved outside the front door of the police station. Zeke was right on her heels.

"Drunk and disorderly conduct?" she asked in a low voice, pressing the key fob for her SUV. The headlights flashed as the doors unlocked. "That's a class C misdemeanor."

"Better than a felony."

Shaking her head, she opened her door and climbed inside. After her son hopped in, she cranked the engine and pulled out. "How did you manage to get into a fight in a bar when you were supposed to be at work?"

"Had the day off."

"Are you sure you weren't fired?"

He grumbled something under his breath. The only words she caught were curses.

"There you go," he said, "always assuming the worst of me."

Things had never been easy with Ezekiel. But she'd always told herself that it wasn't his fault. Pregnant at sixteen and strong-armed by her parents into marrying the father, another high school kid who she didn't love, she hadn't given Zeke the best start. For three years, she'd tried to make the marriage and the picture of a happy family work until she couldn't pretend any longer. Shuttling her son between the homes of contentious parents hadn't been much better. But when her ex, a police officer, had been killed in the line of duty, Zeke spiraled out of control.

No mother would ever give up on her child, but she didn't know what more she could do, what else she could say to get him on the right path.

If only his father, Zachariah, were still alive. They might not have been good as a couple, but her ex had been great in a crisis.

"Can you drop me off at Grandma's?" he asked.

She expelled a low breath. "Why not your place?"

His place being a single-wide trailer in the Happy Meadows mobile home park.

"They cut off the heat. It's freezing in there at night. And before you get on me about paying my bills, I did. Mailed the payment on time. It must've gotten lost at the post office," he said, staring out the window into the darkness. "I don't know why they can't do their job properly, but it's not my fault."

That was the narrative she'd been telling him his whole life. Nothing bad that happened was ever his fault. Maybe it was time that she changed the story.

"How about I take you home with me?" she asked, softening her tone. It was little more than a rustic cabin in the mountains, but it was cozy and warm, and she had a spare room for him.

He snickered. "So you can yap my ear off about fiscal responsibility and not fighting. No thanks. At least I'll get some peace and quiet with Nana. She doesn't nag me like you do."

His paternal grandmother believed the sun rose and set with him. In her eyes he could do no wrong.

"You'd get plenty of peace and quiet in a jail cell," Willa said with extreme patience.

"I can see you gearing up for a lecture. Spare me. Okay? I'm not in the mood."

Not in the mood? As if she was after being pulled away from her job because he'd gotten himself into trouble. "Let's talk about you taking some responsibility for your actions. You chose to go to the bar and drink." When he should've used the money to pay his gas bill. "The fight was as much your fault as it was the other guy's."

"How would you know? You weren't there. I can't believe you're defending a stranger instead of sticking up for me. Maybe I had just cause. Way to go to be supportive, Mom."

"No one is justified when alcohol is involved." Far too many drunks have believed otherwise. "And if I wasn't supportive, I would've told them at the station I didn't need another favor and to charge you. Next time they'll book you, take your fingerprints, a mug shot and you'll be in the system forever. Is that what you want?" She took a breath, chiding herself for letting him lure her into that argument. "A class C misdemeanor could get you up to six months in jail and a fine of seven hundred and fifty dollars. What were you thinking?"

Hesitation. "Guess I wasn't thinking. Just feeling."

One honest thing from him. "Zeke? Please tell me you didn't get into a fight over Sheila Sanders."

"Fine. I won't," he snapped, growing even more defensive.

She could wrangle a suspect twice her size into a restraining hold, cuff him, haul him to the station, handle all sorts of verbal abuse, even from colleagues, put a perp in his place with a few well-chosen words, but when it came to her son, she was a pushover. An illogical, emotional move-heaven-and-earth-for-him softie. Her first job was a mother, doing anything to protect him. In her heart, he was still her top priority.

In her head…she had a higher calling as chief of police.

Willa pulled up to his grandmother's house.

"I thought you and Sheila broke up." The girl was trouble, but Zeke wouldn't listen. At least not to his mother.

"We did."

"Then why did you get into a fight over her?"

He clenched his fingers into fists so tight his knuckles popped.

Her gaze fell to his lap. She stared at the tattoo on the back of his left hand—a moon and sun with an eye in the center.

The only time her son had seemed at peace was as a member of the Shining Light. A blessing as well as a curse.

She put her palm on his forearm, her heart aching in her chest. All she wanted was to keep him safe. For him to be happy, healthy and productive. She'd thought she'd lost him to McCoy's cult and when he came back, at first, she'd been relieved. But Zeke had only been filled with more anger and darkness. Drinking. Fighting. As if he was lost.

"What happened to you on the compound?" she asked in a whisper. "Why did you leave?"

More questions sprang to mind. Had he known Beverly Fisher and Leslie Gooding? Had he seen either of them in the last month?

She didn't dare voice her thoughts. Bringing up anything related to the Shining Light only agitated him. This was already pushing it, begging for a conversation, for a peek into his life.

He jerked his arm away. "Stop asking questions I don't want to answer, Mom. It's not like you ever wanted me to stay on the compound anyway. Just let it go." He got out and slammed the door.

Every time she probed into what happened, he clammed up. Those who'd known Beverly had claimed she'd done the same whenever the Shining Light was brought up.

Watching Zeke climb the porch steps, she wished she could let it go like he wanted. Simply forget his past association with the religious movement she didn't understand. Pretend as though he'd never gotten that tattoo.

But the coincidence of her son returning shortly before the murders started had her stomach twisting in a knot.

Chapter Three

Mrs. Gooding dissolved into tears as she hunched over in her chair and dropped her face into her shaking hands. Her husband wrapped an arm around her, trying to comfort her, but it only brought tears to his own eyes.

Daniel nodded to Deputy Ashley Russo, who he had waiting in the corridor for this very purpose. She swept inside and helped Mrs. Gooding up and out of the office, shutting the door behind them. The grieving mother's sobs echoed in the hall.

"I'm sorry," Mr. Gooding said. "I thought my wife would be able to make it through this interview."

"You have absolutely nothing to apologize for." Willa moved from her seat beside Daniel around the desk to sit next to the distraught father. "You've suffered a horrible loss."

"We'll do our best to get you out of here as quickly as possible," Daniel said, and Mr.

Gooding nodded. "With Leslie being from Cheyenne, how did she first come into contact with the Shining Light?"

"Her grandparents live in Evanston. She's been taking the bus from Cheyenne over there every summer for the last eight years. The bus stops here in Laramie. That's where those kookie people from the cult got to her."

Willa nodded. "It's one of their top recruiting spots. I think it's because so many who are unhoused hang around the area. There are no homeless shelters in Laramie, leaving them vulnerable to predators like the Shining Light. That's also the place where we have the most transients passing through, giving them exposure to people."

Once a month, Daniel had seen them, about fifty or so, wearing Shining Light T-shirts, spreading the word about their religious movement around town, handing out fliers, offering food and shelter to those in need.

"I guess she got curious." Mr. Gooding shrugged. "They filled her head with all sorts of nonsense. Brainwashed her. Instead of going to her grandparents, she ended up on the compound this summer. She joined. Took her *vows*, as if she was marrying the commune," he said with disgust. "Became Lila Starlight, like the name we had given her wasn't good enough anymore."

"Why did she leave the movement?" Willa asked.

Daniel supposed it must have been something compelling to break through the brainwashing.

"She'd been saving up to go to the university," Gooding said. "The time it was taking discouraged her, so we agreed to pay for it. We told her that if she gave college a try, just one year, and didn't like it that we would support her going back to those people. We even took out a second mortgage on our house for the school tuition. The one thing we couldn't get her was a car, but she agreed…on one condition. If, after a year of school, she chose the Shining Light instead, we'd give them a sizable donation."

Daniel exchanged a look with Willa. There hadn't been any mention of money in the statement they'd given the detective. "How sizable?" he asked.

"Ten thousand dollars. Half of one year's tuition."

Willa gave a low whistle. "That's quite a lot. And the commune agreed that they would let her return, if that was what she wanted?"

"I guess so. Leslie seemed pretty certain that it wouldn't be a problem."

Her brow furrowed, and Daniel made a note to circle back around to find out what troubled Willa about that later once they finished with Mr. Gooding.

"Was Leslie taking school seriously?" she asked.

"I think so. She was doing great on her exams. Studied hard. Socialized and went to parties on campus, like we hoped she would. She even joined the track team." He broke down crying. "She'd readjusted to normal life. We thought we had our little girl back."

Daniel handed him more tissues. "Do you know where she liked to go running?"

"Around campus for a quick jog." Gooding dabbed at his eyes. "For anything longer, she preferred the trails through the foothills of the Elk Horn range."

The foothills were close to where they'd found her body. Daniel leaned forward, resting his forearms on the desk. "Did she ever go running at night?"

"Sometimes. But you said her time of death was after midnight. She wouldn't have gone running that late."

"If she didn't have a vehicle, how did she get around town?" Willa asked.

"The public transportation bus service offered by the university, Secure Ride."

"I'm familiar with it," Daniel said. "It's free and operates until two in the morning and goes anywhere in town. She could've gotten to the Elk Horn trail easily depending on where she was dropped off and whether she was running. Riders can use an app, but we didn't find her phone." He'd check with dispatch to see if she scheduled a ride for the night.

"Did she mention a boyfriend?" Willa asked. "A guy that she spent time together with, or anyone she was having trouble with?"

"No. She wasn't dating anyone to our knowledge. She was a sweet kid who got along with everyone." Mr. Gooding straightened. "Are you saying that someone she knew killed her?"

It was not only possible, but likely. Stranger homicide was extremely rare. "Women are far more likely to be murdered by a man known to them than a stranger." Daniel didn't mention that it was also possible that they were dealing with a serial killer.

What they knew for certain was that both women had been between nineteen and twenty-two, with dark hair, slender builds, and had been former members of the Shining Light.

"Thank you for taking the time to speak

with us in person," Willa said. "Where are you staying in town?"

"At the Quenby Bed and Breakfast. We'll be there until we can take our daughter home." Mr. Gooding looked between them with glassy eyes. "When can we see her?"

"Later today." Daniel stood. "I'll have Deputy Russo stop by the B and B. She can take you over to the morgue when it's time."

Somberly, Mr. Gooding rose from his chair. "Please, find who did this and make them pay."

Willa put a hand on his shoulder. "We'll do everything in our power to bring Leslie's murderer to justice."

He nodded and left the office.

The weight on Daniel's shoulders only seemed to get heavier. He could still hear Mrs. Gooding's wailing in his ears and see the devastated look on her face. No one wanted to force a parent to rehash their child's final days, but it came with the job. Such interviews had to be conducted sensitively, with compassion.

Now that they were alone, Willa's placid expression gave way, like a mask slipping. She looked at him, stricken. They were both feeling a bit raw.

For a few heartbeats neither of them said anything, as though they weren't ready to move on from the Goodings misery quite so quickly.

Daniel sat and reviewed his notes. Finally, he broke the silence. "When Mr. Gooding mentioned that his daughter would be allowed to go back to the compound if she decided school wasn't for her, you looked skeptical. Why?"

Willa paced in the office. "After you take your vows, if you decide to leave, they consider you one of the Fallen. They don't welcome you back with open arms according to their PR rep."

"Maybe they do if your parents are writing a check for ten grand."

Stopping, she stood still, her gaze meeting his. "I wonder if they've done that before."

"Let someone come back for a price?"

"Yeah." Willa folded her arms. "What if McCoy realized that Leslie was readjusting and might not return with all that money?"

"You're thinking motive. But what about Fisher? You weren't able to track down any family and she was living on the streets. No potential loss of cash with her."

"It's possible one of his acolytes, a real zealot who wasn't happy about people leaving, specifically women, took matters into his own hands. It is a patriarchal religious movement."

His cell phone buzzed on his desk, and he

grabbed it. "Autopsy results on Leslie Gooding." He turned to his computer. "I'll pull it up here. We can look at it together," he said, motioning for her to take the seat beside him.

For some reason, she hesitated.

WILLA STARED AT the chair Daniel had hauled around the desk next to his earlier—a gesture to communicate to the Goodings that they were equals, partners, on this case, even if they happened to be in his office. She considered sitting there, close enough to catch the scent of cinnamon and cedar. Close enough to feel his body heat.

Whether he was clean-shaven or had a day's worth of stubble covering his masculine jaw, like now, there was no denying he was a handsome hunk. Smooth brown skin. High cheekbones. His eyes always cool and direct. Her gaze dropped to his full, sexy lips, and she remembered his kisses. On her mouth, her cheeks, her neck, diving lower...

She cleared her throat as well as her head. "I'm good. What does it say?" she asked.

A narrow groove appeared between his eyebrows as he studied her. She swiveled on her heel, turning her back to him, and faced the bullpen. On a side table was a copy of the *Laramie Gazette*. The latest murder was on the front page along with an image of the Shining Light symbol.

There were a lot of people who either didn't understand the religious movement, such as her, or who simply didn't like them, or were afraid of their presence and ever-growing power as their numbers continued to increase. In Willa's experience, it was easy for fear to turn volatile with the right spark.

Two dead women between September and October, only four weeks apart, might just be it.

Clacking on the keyboard filled the air as he pulled up the report. "Know that, know that..." he muttered.

"Time of death?" she wondered.

He read aloud under his breath. "Here we go. Estimated to be between midnight Saturday and two a.m. Sunday."

"Was she raped?"

"No evidence of sexual assault."

The same as Fisher. She stepped closer to the desk, picked up the file, and opened it. "Drugs in her system?" she asked, staring at the photos of Leslie Gooding.

"Preliminary toxicology didn't find a sedative," he said, staring at the screen. "There is strong reason to believe that the victim was impaired at the time of death. Based on the clean wounds, the body was still as she was stabbed. The victim hadn't thrashed or moved about. If something like chloroform was used it would be difficult to detect unless a lethal amount was used."

"That's consistent with the trace amounts of chloroform we found in a tent used by Fisher and explains why there were no defensive wounds or bruising on either. She was probably just waking up when he killed her since her eyes were open." The guy wanted her to know who did this to her. That's why he waited for her to regain some consciousness. "The cut to her throat wasn't the fatal one. It was done postmortem, right?"

"Yes. Immediate cause of death was exsanguination. Four stab wounds to the chest, some deeper than others. Three missed the heart by millimeters. One didn't."

Frustration welled inside her as she set the pictures down. "Any DNA?"

"Nothing significant under the nails or on the body."

"Once again, no blood, no hair, no saliva, no semen, no prints." No DNA. "But he took his time with her and left quite a mess. What does that say to you?" She turned toward him.

"The killer was careful," Daniel said. "Used

gloves. Probably wore something to cover his clothing and possibly his hair."

"How long did he watch both of them, planning this?" It was a rhetorical question that neither of them could answer. What if he was stalking his next victim right now?

With a knock, the door to the office opened. Peggy Tuckett walked in, carrying a pot of coffee. "Figured you two could use a refill," she said, sympathetically. The office manager looked to be in her late seventies, with salt-and-pepper hair and hazel eyes.

"Thank you," Willa said, going to the desk and picking up her mug. "I could definitely use some more hot coffee."

Peggy topped up her cup, and then she went around and did the same for Daniel. "Let me know if you need anything else." She started to leave when her gaze shifted to the photos on the desk, and she stopped. Two deep lines appeared between Peggy's brows as she stared at the victim.

"What is it?" Daniel asked.

"This reminds me of a cold case we had a few years back," Peggy said, peering closer at the pictures. "Four dead women. Tied up like that. Stabbed. No suspects. One day, the murders simply stopped."

Willa cupped her mug with both hands. "How long ago was that?"

"I can't say for certain," Peggy said, with a one-shoulder shrug. "Maybe four or five years."

Relief trickled through Willa. If the killer had done this before, then…

Deep down she knew that despite Zeke's rage at the world, her son wasn't capable of this. Not of murdering anyone.

She glanced up and found Daniel studying her. Quickly, she schooled her features.

"Who was on the case?" Daniel asked Peggy with his keen gaze still on Willa.

"The previous sheriff. Jim Ames. He worked it alone. But the more time that passed, the less effort he put into it."

"Nothing came up in ViCAP." There was no mistaking the frustration in his voice.

Peggy sighed. "Ames never used it to my knowledge."

The database was designed specifically to analyze information about homicides that were known or suspected to be part of series, apparently random, motiveless, or sexually oriented. Though it wasn't a requirement where no sexual assault had occurred, Ames should have made more of an effort to input the cases.

Daniel muttered something under his breath,

and she caught a curse. "I should've let Holden look at the file like he wanted to last night. He was here back when Ames had the case."

"I wonder why the medical examiner didn't mention the similarities," Willa said, thinking aloud.

"That ME only started three years ago and wouldn't have performed those autopsies, but I can pull up the files for you," Peggy offered.

"I've got it," Daniel said, clacking away on the keyboard, not wasting any time.

"I'll place an order for lunch over at Delgado's Bar and Grill. Sandwiches all right?" Peggy asked.

With a grunt, Daniel nodded. "I'll take a Reuben, please."

"Any kind of soup and a Caesar salad with grilled chicken for me." Willa wished she had an office manager as efficient and thoughtful as Peggy. "Thank you," she said.

"Only doing my job." The older woman headed out of the office, closing the door behind her.

"I found it. The murders happened five years ago spanning from November to January. They referred to him as the Holiday Elk Horn Killer since the first one occurred over Thanksgiving weekend and the last on New Year's Eve.

All the bodies were found in and around the Elk Horn Mountains."

Willa stepped closer. "The timeline is shorter. Four murders in three months."

"I'll bring up all the autopsy reports and case files. Want to take a look with me?" Daniel met her gaze. "Promise I won't bite." The corner of his mouth hitched up in a grin that chased away her hesitation.

The quiet, straightforward way about him was one of the things she'd enjoyed most. Over the years, she'd had her fill of pushy Neanderthals that only made her want to push back in return. Her father. Her ex-husband. Daniel didn't fit that mold. He didn't find the need to be a domineering alpha male, even though he was in a position of power.

She slid into the seat next to him. "Might be faster if you let me use Holden's computer since he's out. We can split up the reports."

"If that'll suit you. Then again, it might be easier to compare and discuss if we're in the same office," he countered, and it was hard to disagree.

He brought up the autopsy report on the first victim, who had been identified as Tiffany Cummings, and they perused the findings.

"Many of the details seem to match our current cases. Except for…" His voice trailed off as she caught what had stopped him.

"She had a scalp hematoma at the base of the skull like she'd been struck. And bite marks on her neck and shoulder."

He turned to her. "Sorry, about what I said a few minutes ago. It was in poor taste."

"Well, you did promise *not* to bite," she said, "and there was no way for you to know what we'd find in the report."

Daniel smiled at her, and her belly tingled in response. He clicked on the case file, bringing it up on the screen and they scrolled through it.

"Look at that," she said. "All the victims were found about a mile from their vehicles."

"And two tires had been shot out with a .223-caliber bullet."

"He used a high-powered rifle to disable the victims' cars," she said. "And then what? How did they end up one mile away?"

"It's possible the victims didn't realize their tires had been shot out and thought they had simply blown. Unless your ear is trained to recognize the difference in the sounds, it's easy for a civilian to confuse."

She had been shooting since she was ten years old and would know the difference. "Maybe they walked to get help and he got them then." She flicked a glance back toward the bullpen. "One minute." More details that differed from the current case might pop up. She needed to see the cases spread out in front of her. Sometimes if she mapped it, she was able to figure out the why that led to the who.

Willa went to the bullpen and grabbed the standing whiteboard near the wall that she'd spotted. Since it wasn't in use, she commandeered it and rolled it into Daniel's office, then went hunting for markers. Once she had the board set up and had acquired markers from the office supply closet Peggy showed her, she started to make notes about all the victims on the whiteboard.

"Keep going," she said to Daniel. "I'll highlight the differences and then we can fill in everything else we know."

Two hours later they had finished. Stepping back, Willa and Daniel studied what she'd done, including taping up photos of all the victims and one of McCoy centered over the latest ones.

The whiteboard was a good start. "We can add to it as we discover more," she said. For now, the order helped her breathe a little easier.

"It helps me to see everything laid out like this, too. Looking at it, I'm not so sure the killers are the same."

"Copycat?" Willa stared at the board, seeing

the possibility. "But some of the specifics that were never released to the public are identical. The way the women were bound. All with nylon rope. Their wrists tied to tree trunks. Stripped down to their undergarments, but not violated. None of that had been in the papers."

"Although all the victims had been dark-haired, the first set had a wider range of ages, twenty to forty. They were also drugged. Medetomidine was found in their systems whereas as chloroform was used with the latest victims."

The report had stated medetomidine was used in veterinary anesthesia. "Maybe he ran out of the stuff or couldn't get access to it anymore."

"The murders that happened five years ago were more brutal—the hematomas and the bite marks. Why hit them if he had drugged them?"

"He used the drug to slow them down and hit them because he enjoyed it. Maybe he was more passionate about it five years ago because he was just getting started. Leaving behind his DNA was sloppy. Perhaps he learned, evolved."

"The first set of victims were killed over the holidays. None on a full moon. Why the five-year break? Why start targeting women from the Shining Light?" Daniel asked. "Why move from the Elk Horn Mountains to their backyard?"

"Let's say it's the same guy. What if he stopped killing because he joined the Shining Light and started up again because they kicked him out? It would explain the break and provide motive for targeting the new victims. Also, the two areas where the bodies were found aren't that far apart." She pulled a map and marked where all the bodies had been discovered. "The location of the last victim from five years ago is only three miles from Leslie Gooding."

"I've got your lunch order." They turned to see Mercy McCoy—Marshall McCoy's daughter, who recently left the movement and had become one of the Fallen—standing at the door to the office, holding up a bag of food from Delgado's where she now worked.

Willa turned the board around to hide their notes.

"They won't talk, but I think we have someone else who will," Daniel said, looking at Mercy.

McCoy's daughter knew the inner workings, understood the Shining Light's beliefs, but was no longer a believer. Her boyfriend had been the federal agent targeted last month by domestic terrorists who had been linked to her father.

If there was anyone who might be willing to tell them the truth about the cult, it was her. In fact, she might be their greatest resource of information from the inside.

"Thanks," Daniel said, taking the lunch delivery from her. "Would you happen to have a few minutes you could spare?"

"This is a busy time of day at the bar and grill."

"It's important," Willa said. "We just have a few questions."

"Okay. I guess I could use my break." Mercy gave a polite smile. "Questions about what?"

"Please, take a seat." Daniel motioned to a chair. "We were hoping you could help us out with a case."

Mercy sat, folding her hands in her lap. "The one in the paper about the victims who were former Shining Light members?"

"Yes." Willa nodded. "Did you know Beverly Fisher and Leslie Gooding? They went by Blue and Lila Starlight on the compound."

"I did, but Blue left the commune a while ago. Back in February. And Lila wasn't with us long either. She left in July. Two months before me."

Something struck Willa. "You said that Lila wasn't with the community long *either*. How long were they members?"

"Blue was with us for a year and a half, but she didn't become a member until January. Weeks later she left. Whereas Lila came to us around March, I think, and took her vows right away. Then was gone soon after, too. The paper said that they were stabbed." Mercy tensed as she wrung her hands. "Did they suffer?"

Willa didn't want to lie, but they didn't need to burden Mercy with the truth. The young woman had an innocent quality about her, probably from her sheltered life on the compound. In the past month that she'd been free, she'd blossomed while retaining her kindness, extraordinary empathy and positive outlook that Willa envied. She didn't want to be the one to taint that.

"No," Daniel said, "they didn't."

"When did they die?" Mercy asked. "The *Gazette* was vague. It simply stated that Blue had been killed last month. And Lila yesterday?"

Willa nodded. "Leslie Gooding was murdered between midnight Saturday and two a.m. Sunday. Beverly Fisher on September 19 between ten p.m. and midnight."

"Oh, my God, that's the same day I left the compound for good." Her gaze fell and roamed like she was thinking.

"What is it?" Willa drew closer. "If something occurred to you, no matter how small you think it, you should tell us."

Mercy chewed on her lower lip. "It's only that the day I left there was a full moon. There was one on Sunday, too."

Daniel took out a notepad. "Is there a significance to that?"

"For the Shining Light, definitely." Mercy nodded. "We, I mean they believe that a full moon is about transformation, where the seeds planted on the new moon are brought to fruition. But last month on the 19th was a supercharged version. A time for one thing to end and something else, something big to begin."

Was Fisher's murder the beginning of a killing spree?

Daniel stopped writing. "Do you know why Blue and Lila decided to no longer be a part of the movement?"

Shaking her head, Mercy pushed her blond hair back behind an ear. "My father didn't want me to be a part of any dealings with the process of the Fallen. Looking back, I wonder if he thought it might encourage me to leave. Feed into my doubts. Do you know why they were killed? Is it because they used to be Starlights?" Concern riddled her face.

Daniel sat on the edge of the desk, facing

the young woman. "That's what we're trying to figure out."

"We believe you can provide answers that we desperately need," Willa said. "Your father refused to speak to me. I got the runaround from the PR person, Sophia Starlight."

Mercy laughed bitterly. "PR. What a joke. Sophia is my father's fiancée. Anything she told you came directly from him."

"Are there any circumstances in which your father would let someone go and then agree to take them back?" Willa asked.

"Penumbroyage. It's when a person from sixteen to twenty-four is allowed a year away before taking their vows."

Daniel looked at Willa, the same thought probably going through their heads. "What about after taking their vows?" he asked.

"No. It's forbidden. Someone would be considered the Fallen."

Willa still had her doubts. "Has your father ever accepted money to take back someone who was once Fallen?"

Mercy's gaze fell to her lap, her body tensing.

Willa put a hand on her shoulder. "You can talk to us without fear of reprisals from your father or anyone else on the compound."

"It's not that. I'm not afraid of my father.

But I can't honestly say what line he wouldn't cross when it comes to funding and protecting the commune. Anything is possible."

"Do you know anyone on the compound who might be fanatical enough to kill two women because they left?" Daniel asked.

"The one person who would have been, tried to kill me. But he's dead."

Willa nodded, understanding. The LPD had handled the case. "Is there anyone on the compound who can tell us more about Blue and Lila's time there? Why they left? If they had upset anyone in the commune?"

"*Can* and *will* are two different things. Most of them won't betray my father by answering your questions honestly," Mercy said, and Willa wanted to get McCoy on obstruction so badly it was like an itch under her skin, but it would be hard to prove. "His hold on them is too strong."

"Most, but not all." Willa pinned Mercy with a stare. "Who might talk?"

The young woman's bright blue gaze bounced between them. "Arlo. She's an educator at the compound and an elder on the council. She's the only one to ever question my father when no one else would. They had an argument not long ago about how the Shining Light got their tax-exemption status as a religious organization. She was upset that he was hurting former members somehow to achieve it."

"Hurting them in what way?" Daniel asked.

Mercy shrugged. "Arlo might tell you."

"Might?" Willa studied Mercy. "Is there any way we can persuade her?"

Her gaze fell. "Tell her you spoke to me. That I left because...my father is the true devil. A liar. Evil. His darkness has tainted everything he's built," she said as Daniel took furious notes, "and will one day be destroyed because of his wickedness. One way or another."

Willa could tell it wasn't easy for Mercy to say those things.

"But questioning her in front of others would only endanger her," Mercy added.

"There must be some way to get her alone," Willa wondered.

"She participates in the recruitment of new members in town during the new moon. She'll be wearing yellow, the color for educators. Glasses. Gray bob cut. Arlo stands out."

Daniel got up and went to his computer. "When's the next new moon?"

"In fourteen days," Mercy replied before he had a chance to look it up.

Willa groaned in frustration. "We can't wait that long to talk to her."

Mercy's gaze fell, unease creeping through her expression. As Willa thought she might have to gently nudge her to talk, Mercy finally said, "Arlo also leads smaller weekly excursions to neighboring cities. Every Wednesday they leave shortly after sunrise. They take the same route to get to the interstate. But she won't be alone. If you talk to her, others will report it. There might be a better way to find out what you need to know about Blue and Lila. Empyrean," she said, referring to the name acolytes called Marshall McCoy, "keeps meticulous records. Everyone goes through an unburdening session before they take their vows, where they confess their deepest and darkest secrets to him. He records it and has been known to use it against current members as well as former."

"Use it how?" Daniel asked, raising his brows. "Are you talking extortion? Is that how they got their tax-exempt status?"

"I don't know for certain. If I did, I'd tell you, but I wouldn't put it past him. My father isn't a good person. He needs to be stopped."

"Does he also keep records of why people left?" Willa asked.

Mercy met her gaze. "He does, but only on those who were members. Not on the transients who don't take vows. The files are restricted to him and the council of elders. There's a process to someone leaving. They discuss it and document it. Everyone has to approve, but they generally follow Empyrean's lead. The community says their goodbyes and they're driven off the compound."

"Driven?" Daniel stopped writing and looked up from his notepad. "By who?"

"We—they—don't have dedicated drivers. It's always someone from the security team, but they keep a logbook to track it."

"Where are the unburdening records and restricted files kept?" Willa asked.

"In the security building."

Thinking about the prospect that the killer was hiding on the compound, Willa had another question. "Is it possible for someone to stay on the compound without becoming a member indefinitely?"

Mercy considered it. "I suppose, yes, it is. I was there for twenty-four years without taking vows. They don't impose time restrictions on those who come to us as adults. They want people to embrace the Light when they're ready."

"And there's no documentation on a new recruit, someone who hasn't decided?" Daniel asked. "Not even if they were kicked out for doing something wrong?"

Mercy shook her head. "None. They never saw the need for it."

The perfect place and way for a killer to hide, off the grid, no paper trail, no online footprint.

"Thank you," Daniel said. "You've been very helpful."

Mercy bowed her head with a solemn look. "It doesn't feel like it."

"Trust me," Willa said with a nod, "you have." With a witness to attest to the existence of the unburdening tapes, restricted files, and logbook of drivers, they now had enough for a warrant.

Daniel picked up the phone. "I'll get the district attorney to expedite a warrant for us."

Willa nodded in agreement.

DA Allen Jennings had been trying to bring down the Shining Light at least since Willa had taken over as chief of police. She didn't know why he had the group, specifically Marshall McCoy, in his crosshairs, but if anyone could get a judge to sign off on a warrant in less than an hour, day or night, it was him.

"I'll walk you out," Willa said to Mercy.

The young woman rose from her seat, and they left the office, giving Daniel some privacy.

"Thank you again for your assistance. I also

want you to know that we don't believe you have any reason to worry about your safety so far, but it's best to increase your situational awareness and not go anywhere alone at night until we catch the killer." Since Mercy had blond hair and blue eyes, a stark difference to the dark-haired, brown-eyed victims, she doubted that the young woman would become a target. She also had an added layer of protection by living with her boyfriend who was a federal agent.

"I will. If you need anything else, don't hesitate to ask."

A chair scraped against the floor, drawing Willa's attention.

Peggy hopped up and hurried toward her. "You're never going to believe this. There's another body."

Mercy gasped as the words sent a cold chill skittering down Willa's spine.

"Who called it in?" Willa asked.

Peggy grimaced. "Hikers out near the foothills of Elk Horn. They saw vultures circling in the sky, went to check it out, expecting to find the carcass of an animal and found a dead woman instead. One of the hikers called his cousin, a cop on the Laramie PD. The officer checked it out since family was involved even though it was well outside of the city limits."

And a violation of protocol, but Willa kept the thought to herself.

"The officer just called it in," Peggy added, "since it's our jurisdiction and he knew you'd be here at our office."

"I bet she was killed last night." Mercy wrapped her arms around herself like she was suddenly cold. "Before midnight. While there was still a full moon."

"There's one more thing," Peggy said. "The officer stated that the victim didn't have a *tattoo* of the Shining Light from what he could see."

The deviation from the new pattern made Willa's stomach churn. More concerning, two women had lost their lives in the span of less than twenty-four hours, and whoever did this was out there free to kill again.

"But…" Peggy's expression was sober as her voice trailed off, "the symbol had been carved onto her stomach."

Mercy gasped.

The murders had already been gruesome enough. But the carving made her wonder. "On second thought, Mercy, there is one more thing you can do. Come with us and see if you can identify the woman."

"If she doesn't have a tattoo, I'm not sure how much use I'll be, but I'll come if you want me to. It's just they're expecting me back at Delgado's."

"I'll call them. Work it out so it doesn't impact your job. Thank you." Her gut told her there might be a connection between the victim and the cult. Then again it could be nothing more than wishful thinking. Either way, Mercy would help them to establish or eliminate a link.

Willa was betting on the former.

Chapter Four

Taking the camera from Pruitt, Daniel headed to the grove of trees, where Willa waited alongside Mercy. From there, they were able to see the yellow crime scene tape draped around trees that cordoned off the perimeter and the officers canvassing the area, but not the body.

Willa said something to the young woman, who nodded in reply, and broke off, meeting him before he made it within earshot of Mercy. "Is it like the last two?" she asked.

"Sort of. The one change was instead of a tattoo there was the carving. Pruitt estimates the time of death to be between seven p.m. and midnight yesterday. She was right," he said, hiking his chin toward Mercy. "The victim was killed during the full moon. Same type of stab wounds as well as a cut across the throat."

"Whoever the killer is," Willa said, "he's familiar with the Shining Light's beliefs. Mercy said the back gate to the compound is less than three miles from here. I asked her if any Starlight can use one of the compound vehicles." Willa shook her head no. "But any of them can take a horse out for a ride."

"We'll have to conduct a wider search for horse tracks."

"Only problem with that is there's a dude ranch two miles due east," she said.

The ranch would offer horseback riding off the property. Any tracks they found might not lead back to the cult's compound.

Tipping her head back, Willa's jaw hardened. "The audacity of this perp to think he can kill two women in one day and get away with it."

"It makes me think of the way he fans their hair out around their head," Daniel said. "Making them a spectacle. As though he's demanding our attention."

"Well, he's got it all right. I don't care how many sleepless nights it takes—we have to catch him before the next full moon."

He nodded in agreement. Next time, the killer might take three lives, escalating the pageantry of these murders. "Let's see if Mercy can ID her," he said.

They started down the slight incline toward her.

"Were you able to get a hold of Rocco?" he

asked, referring to the young woman's boyfriend. Willa had thought it best to contact him.

"Yep. I explained the graphic nature of the pictures that she would see," Willa said, keeping her voice low, "and how it might be hard on Mercy to look at them. He's on the way. One of my officers is out in the woods, near the road to lead him up here."

Mercy stood trembling, her arms wrapped around her stomach like she was trying to hold herself together.

Daniel wished there were a better way to investigate a possible connection to the victim and the cult than involving Mercy any further. But their options were slim, and they were running out of time. He pulled up a picture on the viewfinder. He zoomed in on the dead woman's face, so she didn't have to see any of the gruesome wounds. Still, it would be difficult for a civilian to look at with the victim's eyes open, skin gray, hair deliberately positioned, postmortem. Truth be told, although he'd gotten used to the horror, it never failed to repulse him.

"This won't be easy," Daniel said, in an effort to prepare her. "But it's important that you take your time, okay? We need you to be sure. One way or the other." He turned the viewfinder toward her.

Her jaw unhinged. She rocked back on her heels, the blood draining from her face.

"Take a deep breath." Willa clasped Mercy's shoulders. "Do you recognize her?"

For a long moment, Mercy stood silent and trembling, staring at the horrid image.

"Do you recognize her?" Willa repeated gently. "If you're not sure, that's o—"

"Gemma with a *G*." Mercy's voice was barely audible. Her gaze transfixed on the screen. Tears welled in her eyes. "Her name is Gemma Chavez. Oh, my…" She put a hand over her mouth. Tears fell, rolling down her cheeks, and Daniel shut off the camera. "I helped recruit her. I think it was last October before the first snow. It was so cold out. She was shivering and I could see the wind cutting right through her. She was still at the compound when I left."

"Was she planning to take her vows?" Daniel asked. "Become a Starlight?"

"I don't know. I don't think so. She seemed like she was biding her time, not really interested in learning about the Light. Is this my fault for encouraging her to come to the compound? Did I make her a target?"

"This is not your fault," Daniel said.

"You aren't responsible for the sick actions

of another person." Willa patted her back. "Don't you dare blame yourself."

"I think I'm going to be sick." Whirling around, Mercy rushed off, not making it far before she leaned against a tree trunk and retched.

Willa took a few steps in her direction, then they noticed Rocco Sharp hurrying through the woods, escorted by an LPD officer and Deputy Livingston. The ATF agent spotted Mercy and ran to her. He slid a comforting around her, bringing her in to a tight hug.

It was a good thing Willa had the foresight to call Rocco. Mercy would need someone close to her for reassurance and support.

Deputy Livingston approached them. "The warrant came in." He held it up.

Daniel took it and perused it with Willa. "The warrant isn't as wide in scope as I would have liked." He slipped it in the back pocket of his jeans. "The victim's name is Gemma Chavez," he said to Livingston. "Get statements from her family and friends. See if they know why she lived on the compound. Get them to confirm dates. See if she had any intention of taking her vows."

Livingston nodded. "I'm on it."

"Let's go knock on McCoy's door," Willa said. "This time it'll go much differently."

Indeed, it would. Even if Marshall McCoy tried to stonewall, now they'd at least get access to some of his records.

They made their way through the woods back to his vehicle. Driving up to the compound, they passed protesters that had gathered near the front gate. The group was small, no more than ten people. But they were loud. They held signs that read STOP KILLING WOMEN WHO REJECT YOU and CULTY MURDERERS. Through bullhorns they chanted, "Shining Light, you are a blight!"

Daniel pulled up beside the guardhouse and rolled down his window.

"Afternoon," said the armed guard. "May the Light shine upon you."

Not sure how to respond to the greeting, Daniel simply nodded. "Sheriff Clark," he said, loud enough for the security guard to hear him and pointing to the star fastened to his shirt, "and chief of police Nelson here to speak with Marshall McCoy."

"*Empyrean* is unavailable unless you have an appointment or a warrant."

Lucky for them they had both. "We have an appointment. Chief Nelson called ahead earlier and notified your PR rep that we'd be stopping by."

The guard nodded. He went back inside the

guardhouse and made a call. The guy had to cover his other ear just to hear over the protesters. After a minute, he returned. "You can go on up to Light House. It's the main building at the top of the hill. Security will be waiting for you." He hit a button and the wrought iron gate swung open.

Daniel tipped his hat in thanks, and they proceeded up the long driveway. In the late afternoon light, the large building made of glass and steel gleamed like something straight out of a modern fairy tale.

"They're completely self-sufficient here," Willa said, looking out the window. "Sophia gave me the spiel about how they grow all their own food, make most of their clothing and furniture."

"Wow. Really?"

More guards were scattered across the grounds. All had handguns holstered to their hips or rifles slung over their shoulders. Agent Rocco Sharp had uncovered arsenal on this compound, but it turned out that none of their weapons were illegal, and they had enough to arm a small army.

"They're also vegetarians," Willa added. "Or vegans. I forget which."

"Ashley, Deputy Russo, has been here once before. She told me that they use Light House for everything from celebrations and meetings, to communal meals. But only McCoy lives here. His children used to." He parked where a security guard indicated in front of the building, and they climbed out.

The chanting from the other side of the gate could easily be heard.

"Follow me." The guard led the way up the wide stone steps.

Neighboring the main house was a ten-bay detached garage. A couple of dual-sport motorcycles and one white van with their symbol painted on the side were out front.

The guard opened the door, letting them in. "Please wait here for Empyrean. He'll be with you shortly." Then he closed it, leaving them alone.

"Tight security," Daniel whispered, in case anyone was lurking out of sight, eavesdropping.

"I get having armed security at the guardhouse, but it's odd to have so many guards on the compound when people are supposedly free to leave whenever they want, don't you think?" she asked.

He took off his Stetson while Willa left hers on. "I agree. It is."

Standing in the impressive two-story foyer of Light House, Daniel looked around. He took in the entryway of polished steel and ten-foot-high windows that spanned the walls, the gleaming chandelier and veined marble floor. A lot of money had been poured into this building and the entire compound, a hundred acres surrounded by a brick wall, complete with a guardhouse and fancy wrought iron gate.

"Big bucks paid for all this," Willa whispered, echoing his thoughts, and he gave a subtle nod. "And it's spotless. You could eat off the floor. I wonder how many people it takes to keep this place looking so pristine."

"My apologies for the delay." Marshall McCoy came down the hallway, wearing a white suit that had been impeccably tailored. He was accompanied by a bald middle-aged man, dressed in a yellow tunic and matching pants and a woman in her early twenties who wore a green dress.

Daniel had learned the Shining Light had a color system to represent a person's function in the community. Educators wore yellow. The creative types dressed in orange. Gray was for security. The woman in green was an essential worker.

"I was waiting for our community lawyer, Huck Starlight, to join us," McCoy said indicating the bald man. "And Sheriff Clark, this is our PR rep, Sophia. Chief Nelson, I believe you're already acquainted."

Willa flashed a tight smile. "I am indeed."

"If you wouldn't mind removing your shoes before we proceed to my office." McCoy gestured to their boots.

Daniel noticed the others were barefoot. "We can conduct the interview here. We won't be inside Light House long."

McCoy clasped his hands in front of him. "I understand you have questions about the recent murders of two former members."

"That's correct." Daniel was itching to get through the preliminaries. "Do you know why Beverly Fisher and Leslie Gooding decided to leave the community?"

"I believe, after careful consideration on their part, they decided that the Shining Light wasn't the right fit for them."

"Can you be more specific?" Willa asked.

"I don't recall specifics." McCoy pulled on a placating grin. "I have more than five hundred in my flock. Everyone seeking the Light is welcomed here. At times, we take in twenty or more potential recruits a month. We tend to get quite a few young people who have nowhere else to go." His gaze shifted, locking solely on Willa. "Especially those having difficulty at home with judgmental parents who can't accept them as they are. They receive unconditional love here." His smooth smile spread wider, and Daniel couldn't help feeling as though he was missing something. "Not all decide that our way is for them. After they've received rest and nourishment of body, mind and spirit, some choose to move on. I don't commit to memory all their reasons for leaving. If the message of the Light isn't for them, that's fine. In the end, we might have saved a life. No one is held at the compound against their will. Our mission here is to help people. To make the world a better place."

"That's a nice speech," Daniel said. "But let's focus on the victims. There's a third one. We found her three miles from your back gate. Like Beverly and Leslie, she was murdered during the full moon."

McCoy, Huck and Sophia all exchanged guarded glances.

"Any idea why the killer might choose the full moon to act?" Willa asked. "Is there a special significance to the Shining Light?"

Another practiced smile. "I can't imagine what might be going through the mind of a killer. As for the moon, all of its cycles have significance for us," McCoy said, then Huck put a hand on his shoulder and whispered in his ear. "I have no idea why the killer would choose the full moon, but as stated in the *Farmers' Almanac*, it's considered a good time to harvest. Perhaps he got the idea from there. I doubt it has anything to do with us."

"Unlike the victims who have a direct tie to your..." Willa drew in a deep breath but did a great job of hiding the frustration she must have felt. "Religious movement," she said, stopping short of calling it a cult to his face.

The cagey responses were certainly testing Daniel's patience, as well. "The latest victim has been identified as Gemma Chavez. A recruit. She came to the compound a year ago, last October."

"According to whom?" Huck asked.

"One of the Fallen who was here during that time period," Daniel replied.

Huck's jaw hardened.

But McCoy didn't even flinch. "Gemma left us last week after deciding not to take her vows."

"Why did she wait a year?" Daniel asked. "Did something happen?"

"Last month the domestic terrorists who were after agent Rocco Sharp also made a threat against us. For the safety of the commune, I instituted a lockdown. If you've never been through one before, it could be scary. At the same time, my daughter chose to turn her back on the Light and embrace darkness. It instilled serious doubts in Gemma. We tried for three weeks to help her overcome them. Ultimately, fear won over faith because she was weak. And the devil found her out there, where the world is cruel."

"The fact that the latest victim also had a previous connection to your organization will be made public," Willa said.

The easy smile slipped from McCoy's face. "News of the murders has spread throughout the community, putting everyone on edge. As if that weren't enough, now we have protesters, with their bullhorns to ensure their voices carry, thanks to the latest article in the *Gazette*. Nice touch calling him the Starlight Killer."

"Seemed fitting," Willa said.

McCoy stepped closer to her. "The only problem with that is Gemma Chavez was not a Starlight."

"She was one of your recruits," Daniel said. "Lived here as a de facto Starlight for more than a year and her killer carved your symbol onto her torso. I'm inclined to agree with Chief Nelson. It's fitting."

McCoy's Adam's apple started bobbing like he was suddenly nervous. "It's unfortunate to hear that."

Willa cocked her head to the side. "Might be

even more unfortunate if the number of protesters outside continues to grow. It's in your
best interest to cooperate with us unless you
have something to hide."

Every cell in Daniel's body told him that
McCoy had plenty to hide.

"Here I stand." McCoy outstretched his
arms. "Fully cooperating."

"Then you wouldn't mind showing us your
logbook of drivers for the dates Fisher, Gooding and Chavez left the compound and were
dropped off," Daniel said, and McCoy's expression turned deadpan, but Sophia suddenly
looked nervous. "In addition to the unburdening tapes and restricted files detailing why
they left."

McCoy opened his mouth to speak, but
Huck stepped forward, stopping him.

"Not without a warrant," Huck said.

Daniel pulled the document from his back
pocket. "Just so happens we have one."

Glaring, Huck snatched it from his hands
and read it. "The logbook of drivers, yes. A
list of members who joined within the past five
years along with a list of those who became the
Fallen this year." For a minute, he was quiet
as he read the warrant. "But only the audio
recordings of unburdening sessions and files
for the two women who were once members."

Daniel had hoped for greater leeway regarding access to other files, but the district attorney had warned that the judge would view it as a violation of the Fourth Amendment and the right to privacy of the other members, past and current, unless they could show sufficient probable cause. Which they didn't have. Yet.

For now, this would have to suffice.

"We also need a list of everyone over the age of eighteen who has been on the compound for the past four to five years, but hasn't taken vows," Willa said.

Huck scowled. "We don't have any documentation on individuals who are not members. We can't give you what we don't have."

"Surely you know who is and isn't a member and how long they've been with you," Willa insisted.

Huck took McCoy off to the side. The two spoke in hushed tones too low to be overhead. After a moment of deliberation, McCoy nodded, and they came back.

"We are happy to comply," McCoy said. "It will take us some time to get you that list since we have hundreds here. We should have it ready for you in a week."

"You have forty-eight hours, and one more thing." Daniel hooked his thumbs on his duty belt that carried his gun, handcuffs, radio, baton and pepper spray. "Did you agree to let Gooding return to the commune in a year if her parents paid you ten thousand dollars?"

"Now that you mention it, I do recall granting her a form of penumbroyage since she was so young and her faith wavered. One year to fully commit. Though nothing was predicated on money. We do, however, accept all donations with hearts full of joy."

"Isn't that a violation of your rules?" Willa asked. "Since she had already taken her vows."

"I granted her special dispensation. As Empyrean, I have that liberty," he said, clasping his hands, and Daniel found it funny how his memory had suddenly improved after they produced a warrant. "Sophia will take one of you to the security building where we store the recordings and files. Huck will go with the other to the garage. The logbook is in there."

Sophia and Huck slipped on shoes from a mat near the door.

"Sheriff Clark, if you'll come with me," Sophia said.

Daniel glanced at Willa. "Okay by you?" He didn't think it mattered how they divvied up the task, but it was always good to check.

She hesitated a moment. Then she gave her classic tight smile that he'd learned meant she was uneasy or displeased. "Fine with me."

Outside at the bottom of the stairs, they separated. Putting on his hat, Daniel followed Sophia around to the side of the house. He looked over his shoulder and caught Willa glancing back at him. This time he was certain what the look on her face meant. Unease. But he didn't understand what she was worried about.

He lost sight of her and quickened his step to keep up with Sophia, who marched along as though she wanted to get through an unpleasant chore. With light brown hair and eyes, she was attractive, but beneath her artificially sweet exterior was a toughness that made him wonder if she was what his grandmother would have called an old soul. Maybe she was simply a survivor.

Behind the main house, the whole compound opened beyond an expansive meadow. "What are all those buildings?" he asked. One looked like a chapel.

As she explained, she pointed out the barracks for newcomers contemplating becoming members. Beyond that there was the sanctum, which he gathered to be the church, a schoolhouse, a playground filled with kids, then a series of trailers she called the wellness center, as well as communal bathroom facilities.

"Empyrean and I have a private restroom in the main house, where we live together." She put a hand to her belly in that way pregnant women did, though she wasn't showing. "We also have a farm, stables, an apiary, huts that our single members share and small cabins for families on the far side of the compound. These are some of our newest recruits."

They passed a group all dressed in blue, spinning in circles while someone played a drum and another person, wearing yellow, directed them with instructions on breathing and emptying their minds.

"Would it be possible to speak with some of your elders from the council?"

Sophia smiled, but it didn't reach her eyes which narrowed ever so slightly. "Did you have someone particular in mind?"

"No. I just wanted to get the perspective from a council member."

"You spoke with *her*, didn't you? Empyrean's daughter?"

"You mean Mercy?"

Her lips flattened into a grim line as she bowed her head, averting her gaze. "We do not speak the names of the Fallen."

"I'm afraid I'm not at liberty to disclose our confidential sources, but there are a number of Fallen in and around town."

"You're right. There are. But only one with the level of information you used for your warrant." She made a humming sound. "Here we are." She opened the door to a long building with a tin roof. "This is our security hub."

Inside were five guards working at computer stations. As they walked through, he glimpsed a couple of screens. They were monitoring the entire compound. The cameras had been discreetly placed because he hadn't noticed any of them.

A man came out of an office. "Can I help you, Sophia?" he asked while looking at Daniel.

"Sheriff Clark, this is our head of security, Shawn Starlight. Shawn, they have a warrant to take some materials. We're just here to collect them and we'll be out of your way."

"Do you need any assistance?" Shawn asked.

Although he offered assistance, he sounded like he meant protection.

"No, it's okay. Thank you." Sophia led him down a hall to a room. Above the door handle was a keypad. "If you wouldn't mind." She gestured for him to turn around.

He pivoted on his heels. Beeps resounded behind him and a door clicked open. He turned back. "How many people have access to the records in there?"

"Only Empyrean and the six elders on the council."

"And you, don't you mean."

"I've only been given access recently. I'm still adjusting to my new role as Empyrean's assistant and public relations representative."

"Why the change?" he asked, and her expression soured. "If you don't mind me asking."

"When Empyrean lost his children, everything changed."

The last month must've been difficult for those on the compound with all the upheaval. It was possible the events that led to Mercy leaving, the domestic terrorists attacking a federal agent, and McCoy's son dying could have somehow been the catalyst causing the killer to act.

"Has anyone on the compound acted differently since then?"

"No," she said without even taking a second to think about it. "Here are the records."

There were rows of five-drawer file cabinets for current members, those on penumbroyage, and the Fallen. He hoped more information about the victims and why they left might fill in the missing pieces they needed.

He opened the drawer labeled GHIJ in the penumbroyage section. Sure enough, Leslie

Gooding's file was in there. He pulled out the folder. Inside was a thumb drive and a two-page document.

"The audio file of the unburdening session is on the drive, but there should also be a transcript in the folder," Sophia said.

Daniel went to the cabinets designated for the Fallen. They had been categorized by decade then alphabetized. He opened the drawer under DEF and thumbed through the file folders searching for Fisher.

But another name stopped him.

Ezekiel Nelson.

Poring over the logbook in the garage, Willa noticed that one person in particular had been a driver during every recruiting event—the monthly as well as the weekly ones out of town—and dropped off all the Fallen and those who left the community before taking their vows within the last year.

"Why is Fox the only one to have driven those who were no longer a part of the Shining Light off the compound?" she asked Huck and the security guard in charge of the garage.

"All the guards in training do rounds in every area before being assigned primarily to security," the guard said. He had a kind demeanor unlike the stern, stony-faced Huck.

"When he did his time here in the garage, he loved driving and afterward he volunteered so many times I considered him my go-to guy for drop-offs. He still helps me out with maintenance of the vehicles whenever he has a chance."

"What's Fox's real name?" she asked.

Huck's mouth puckered like he was suddenly sucking on a lemon. "That is his *real* name." The offense in his voice was unmistakable.

She wondered what they called her son while he was with them. He'd always hated the name Ezekiel. Surely he'd changed it. Not that it had been Willa's first, second or third choice. His grandparents had picked it from the Old Testament of the Bible and insisted.

"What's his legal name? The one he came to you with?"

The guy looked at Huck, and the lawyer gave his approval with a nod. "Miguel Garcia."

"Where can I find him?"

"Is he in some kind of trouble?" the guard asked. "Fox is a good guy. He wouldn't do anything wrong. Not on purpose. He's always the first to offer help."

"I have some questions for him. No one is in trouble." Not yet, at least.

Another look at Huck. Another nod. "I can radio and ask him to come over."

She saw no good reason to give Fox a heads-up. "That's all right. I prefer you not to radio. We'll go to him. Where is he?"

"At breakfast he mentioned he worked out getting assigned to patrol near the farm today."

"Thank you." She looked at Huck. "Let's go."

"It's a bit of a walk. Ten or fifteen minutes. Do you mind?" Huck asked, as though he was the one who minded. "I don't know if you're in a hurry."

"I can take her over," the guard said, "on one of the motorbikes. If you want to save time, ma'am."

"What's your name?"

"Everyone just calls me Ry."

"I'm ready whenever you are." She looked over at Huck. "We'll need to take the logbook with us but will return it as soon as we can."

Grabbing a set of keys from a hook, Ry headed out of the garage. She trailed behind him. He cranked the engine to one of the motorcycles parked outside.

She swung her leg over and got on the back. Her Buck Budgie—pocketknife—dug into the crease of her pelvis. Compact but sturdy, she never left home without it if she was working.

She adjusted it in her front pocket until she was comfortable. Putting one hand on Ry's shoulder, she held her hat down with the other.

With a rev of the engine, they sped off.

There weren't any paved paths for him to drive on, but the bike didn't have any trouble zipping through the grass. The ride provided an impromptu tour of the compound. She'd been so curious for so long. What did McCoy and his acolytes give her son that she didn't?

They receive unconditional love here.

McCoy's words rang in her ears. Even the sound of the motorcycle's engine couldn't drown it out.

But had he been right? Had they not judged Zeke, not criticized? Had they freed him to be his best self?

Zeke never talked about this place after he'd been kicked out. Not the people, the facilities, what he'd learned. Not even the food.

Only that he no longer ate meat.

Part of her wished she'd been the one to retrieve the audio files and documents. The other part of her knew it was better not to be faced with the temptation of stealing her son's. Crossing that line would change her. A slippery slope leading someplace she didn't want to go.

But when it came to Zeke, lines tended to blur.

As they pulled up to an orchard, Ry slowed the bike and stopped. He turned off the bike, leaving the key in the ignition, and put the kickstand in place.

They both climbed off. She looked around and spotted a man wearing a gray shirt and slacks carrying a basket of apples, at the same time Ry pointed out the same guy.

He was a little older than her son. She guessed twenty-three, maybe twenty-four.

Willa approached him. As she unhooked her badge from her utility belt and held it up, his eyes grew wide, and he went rigid. "Miguel Garcia—*Fox*—I'm Chief Nelson from the LPD. I have a few questions to ask you about Beverly Fisher, Leslie Gooding and Gemma Chavez."

He dropped the basket, spilling apples across the ground, and took off running into the orchard.

Swearing under her breath, Willa almost bolted after him, but then she had a better idea. She ran back to the motorcycle and hopped on. Turning the key in the ignition, she fired up the bike and backed off the center stand.

"Hey!" Ry said. "You can't take that."

Willa took off her hat, shoved it into his chest, and cranked the throttle. She kept one foot on the ground while she pivoted the bike, the backside swinging wildly as she roared off. By the time she could follow, she'd lost sight of him.

Good thing the workers in the orchard gave him away—confused looks, heads swiveling in the direction he'd run.

She sped down the dirt walkway, taking a right through the trees.

There!

He'd gotten farther than she had expected. The guy was fast.

Quick as a fox.

She raced through the orchard after him. He threw a panicked glance over his shoulder, his eyes flaring wide as saucers as he must've realized he couldn't outrun the motorcycle.

Wending around trees, taking sharp turns, she was grateful for the teen years she'd spent off-road racing with her ex, Zach, on the cheap motorbikes he'd fixed up for fun.

Miguel sprinted out of the orchard into a clearing, giving her the opportunity that she needed.

In a wide-open space, there was no contest. She easily caught up to him. "Stop!"

But the kid kept running like his life depended on it.

Slowing the bike, she put her heel down as

she swung the rear end, bumping the guy. He stumbled and fell.

She stopped the dual-sport, staying mounted, and drew her weapon before he could bolt again. "Down on your knees. Hands behind your head."

Once he did as he was told, she climbed off the bike and unhooked her handcuffs from her duty belt. "Since you ran, we get to have our little Q and A down at the station."

Chapter Five

"Miguel," Daniel said, "let's talk about your previous association to Beverly Fisher, Leslie Gooding and Gemma Chavez." He set down a picture of each deceased woman on the table inside the sheriff's interrogation room and slid them in front of the suspect.

"I—I—I didn't associate with them," he said. "Not really." Putting his unrestrained hands on the table, Miguel lowered his head and looked at the pictures. "Oh, God. I could never do something like this. I would never hurt anyone."

Huck, seated beside him, shoved the photos away.

"Beverly was on the compound for a year and a half," Willa said. "Gemma for twelve months. Leslie for four. Do you expect us to believe that you didn't interact with them at all the entire time until the day they left?"

"I might have talked to them in the dining

hall in passing, but I always sat with the security team. Maybe during one of our celebrations or some other event we might have spoken or something, but that's the extent of it."

Others on the compound had confirmed as much when Daniel had asked around after Willa had put Miguel in the SUV. It's possible they were covering for him, in an effort to protect their image of the Shining Light, but looking at Miguel now, Daniel wasn't quite sure that they were lying. The kid was scared. He didn't strike him as a murderer.

Then again, far too many serial killers came across as normal. Likeable. Twenty-four-year-old Miguel Garcia was both. There was also the fact that he had a record in Idaho. For rape.

"You love being a member of the Shining Light, don't you?" Willa asked, and he nodded. "Why?"

"It's safe for everyone. They don't judge your past. They help you be your best self. We're a community. We look out for each other. Protect one another."

"Even lie to protect a Starlight?" Willa leaned forward. "Maybe even kill to preserve the reputation of the Shining Light?"

Miguel jerked backward, a horrified expression on his face.

"You don't have to answer that," Huck said.

"No, I want to. We walk the path of truth and atone for our transgressions."

"Tell us about the last time you saw each of the victims," Daniel said.

"When someone leaves our community, we usually drop them off at the main bus station in town, after lunch, with their bellies full. With Blue and Gemma, it was different. Blue was the only person I dropped off the entire month of February. People don't leave by choice during the dead of winter. I was told to take her to the church that's across the road from the bus station. And it was right before dinner."

Daniel made a note of it. "Who told you and why?"

Miguel cast a furtive glance at Huck. The older man whispered in his ear.

"Empyrean," Miguel said. "He didn't give me a reason. But I remember that Blue looked sick. She was really pale, sweaty, shaking like she had tremors or something."

Daniel glanced at Willa, but she was entirely focused on Miguel.

Huck put a hand on his shoulder. "You don't have to elaborate," he said in a low voice. "Just answer the question. Keep it simple."

"What about the other two?" she asked. None of the fire had left her tone.

"I don't really remember Gemma, other than

she was nice and didn't seem as if she was taking things seriously."

Willa cocked her head to the side. "How would you know if you didn't associate with her?"

"Folks whispered about it. During the winter months we get a lot of people looking for a warm bed and a hot meal. There's a pattern to the drifters. People pick up on it. Most weren't surprised when she said her goodbyes."

"Were you surprised?" Daniel wondered.

"Kind of. The ones like her, who aren't serious, usually leave in spring or summer. Not as it's starting to get cold. She wanted out really bad the day I dropped her off and she didn't want to wait until after lunch."

Which begged the question, why did she hightail it out of there then? Had something or someone scared her enough to make her leave?

"And Leslie?" Willa asked.

"I remember Lila. I was sad because she had just committed to the Shining Light and then she was leaving all of a sudden, but she wasn't unhappy."

Willa propped her elbows on the table and steepled her fingers. "Were you sad? Sure you weren't angry she left? Angry enough that you'd rather see her dead than living in darkness?"

According to Mercy, that's how they saw the Fallen, as cast out of the Light into the darkness.

Huck's green eyes narrowed to slits. "My client has already stated his feelings."

"I didn't kill anyone," Miguel said. "I thought—we all thought—she was one of us. Then something happened. I don't know what. Next thing I know I was told to drop her off. She talked the entire ride to a couple of other people who decided they didn't want to stay at the commune, telling them she was going to college to make her parents happy. Before she got out of the van, she told me that I'd see her again when she rejoined our family next summer."

Huck put a hand on his shoulder. "Brevity is best."

"What?" Miguel asked the lawyer. "I was just trying to explain that it didn't make any sense to me. I said goodbye and hoped she'd come back to us. I was sad. Not angry."

"Maybe you hit on Beverly, Gemma and Leslie as you drove them," Willa said, "and they didn't appreciate your advances. So you killed them to make them pay for rejecting you."

Since Miguel had a conviction of rape, Willa was playing the right angle with him. Bad cop who thought the suspect had an issue with women.

"It's okay," Daniel said in a softer tone, playing good cop. "You can tell us if things got out of hand and something happened that you didn't intend."

"No way, sir." Miguel shook his head. "I didn't kill those ladies."

Huck took a deep breath. "Chief Nelson, Sheriff Clark, suppositions are not questions. We're done here."

"I only have three more questions." Willa cut her gaze from the lawyer back to Miguel. "Where were you from midnight Saturday to two a.m. Sunday and last night from seven to midnight?"

Daniel wasn't surprised she hadn't asked him about September 19 since the compound had gone into lockdown that night. Anybody with a half a brain, would have claimed that was his alibi whether or not it was true.

"At the compound," Miguel said. "Saturday night I was asleep. I have three roommates who saw me."

Didn't mean he didn't get up while they were also sleeping soundly and sneak out. If the killer was living in the commune, then he was smart enough to have found a way to get out undetected.

"Last night was our full moon celebration," Miguel said. "Dinner was done around seven thirty. We all went to the sanctum and listened to a homily. Afterward, we went around and gave thanks and then we went out to the quad. Danced and sang under the full moon until midnight."

"What was the homily about?" Daniel asked. If he was there, he'd be able to give specifics.

"Empyrean spoke on giving thanks for our ordeals because they're like sandpaper, refining us, making us better. It was inspiring. Uplifting."

"With five hundred members it must be easy for someone to slip away unnoticed," Daniel wondered.

"I suppose." Miguel nodded. "But I danced with Maria most of the night. Empyrean matched us as a couple this summer. She works in the orchard. That's why I requested a work assignment there today. And after the full moon ceremony, I helped the musicians put away their instruments in storage."

"Countless members would have seen him last night," Huck added in a tone implying that Miguel's alibi was solid.

"Then why did you run?" Willa asked.

"Because…" He lowered his head. "I knew this would happen. That you wouldn't listen to me. That you wouldn't believe me. That you wouldn't care about the truth." He glanced up at Daniel with watery brown eyes. "I thought you would be different, but I guess not."

"Why did you think that?"

"You're a Black guy. I'm a brown Hispanic, we don't always get a fair shake."

Daniel had faced his share of struggles. Sometimes people judged him based on the color of his skin before they got to know him as a person, but these two situations were not the same. "That's true. But you ran from an officer of the law after she stated she only wanted to ask questions. Guilty people do that. And you have a record for rape. This doesn't look good for you."

"It was statutory rape," Huck clarified.

"We were both in high school. I was eighteen. My girlfriend was sixteen. And white. Her parents didn't think I was suitable," Miguel said. "They tried to break us up, but Jasmine and I wanted to be together. They went to the cops and had me charged. In Idaho, statutory rape is simply rape. Even though Jasmine made a statement on my behalf and I was an honor roll student, I ending up serving three years. Three. After I was released, I was put on the sexual offender registry. Do you have any idea how hard it was for me to get a job?

An apartment? I was like a pariah when people found out. Except at the Shining Light." He looked at Willa. "I'm sorry I ran, really, I am. I freaked, but that doesn't mean I'm guilty. Please, I didn't do this."

Daniel believed him. One thing for certain, they could eliminate him as the killer in the cold case murders five years ago because Miguel was sitting in an Idaho prison. For another, others on the compound would back his alibi.

"What's your final question for my client, Chief Nelson?"

"Foxes are predators. Is that why you chose the name?" she asked.

The guy hunched over, a defeated expression sweeping over his face. "Did you know young foxes are preyed upon by eagles and coyotes? The adult ones are attacked by larger animals, bears, mountain lions. They're fast, but they can't outrun a wolf. The biggest predator to a fox is humans."

Now even Daniel was curious. "Then why Fox?"

"When I was younger, I got obsessed with reruns of the show *X-Files*. I always thought the name Fox Mulder was cool. The Shining Light gave me a chance to forget my past. To reinvent myself. To accept me as the Light would have me be."

Daniel's heart broke a little for the guy if the rest of his story checked out.

Willa leaned over and whispered, "Hallway."

He followed her out of the room and closed the door. "I don't think he did it."

"Neither do I." She put her hands on her hips. "But I want to verify his story about what happened in Idaho."

"Of course." They needed to dot every *i* and cross all their *t*s.

She turned, heading toward the office, and he caught her arm, stopping her.

"Who is Ezekiel Nelson?"

Stiffening, she schooled her features. "I should have mentioned it sooner, as soon as I saw what was granted in the warrant, but I didn't know how to bring it up."

He wished like hell that whatever she was about to say she'd told him two years ago. Not now because she felt boxed in and had no other choice. "Just tell me. Who is he?"

She shifted her gaze before meeting his as though she was considering telling him a lie. But with a shake of her head, she said, "Zeke is my son."

Daniel didn't see that one coming. He'd

assumed a brother, uncle, possibly a cousin. "After you verify Miguel's story, we need to talk."

"THANK YOU FOR your time answering my questions," Willa said over the phone to Jasmine Emmer.

"Anything for Miguel. How is he? I mean, is he happy, healthy?"

"Yes. He's doing well."

"That's nice to know after what my parents put him through. At the time, they didn't believe me when I told them that he was the love of my life. But it's still true. I think about him every day. Is he married?"

"I believe he's dating someone." Willa wasn't sure how the matchmaking worked.

"Oh." Disappointment resonated in Jasmine's voice. "Good for him. Well, I was happy to help."

"Have a good day." Willa hung up.

Miguel's story was not only true it was heartbreaking. Years ago, he'd been treated unfairly, robbed of three years of his life, for loving the wrong person. But Willa didn't regret getting tough during questioning. That was the job, to push and poke and see if they got a break. They still had a killer to find before he struck again.

Daniel came back into his office and closed the door. "The dispatch from Secure Ride at the university stated that Leslie requested a ride through the mobile app, pickup point the far side of town at seven p.m. Saturday. I figured that's where she would have most likely been if she was coming back from a run at Elk Horn. But then she was a no-show when the driver arrived."

"Because the killer got to her first. Used the chloroform and waited until the time was right."

"Campus police finally tracked down her roommate. The girl has been sleeping at her boyfriend's, but she crossed paths with Leslie on Saturday evening. She came back to get some clothes and Leslie was heading out for a run."

"If the killer is someone on the compound, the full moon event would have been the perfect distraction to disappear, especially if he's a loner that no one would miss."

Daniel mulled that over. "But Saturday night would've been difficult."

"Difficult, sure." She put her feet up on the edge of his desk and rested back in her chair. "Not impossible. Especially if McCoy sanctioned the murders. What if the Holiday Elk Horn Killer joined the Shining Light, unburdened about his taste for blood, and McCoy asked him to do this with his blessing?"

"That's a big leap."

"The murders didn't start up again until after his heir apparent, Mercy, chose the outside world over the one she had been raised in. Rejected her father and the religious movement he started in front of the entire commune. I'm sure it caused doubt to spread like a disease throughout his flock. Killing a few nonbelievers who had turned their backs on the cult, preaching the devil took them, might be his way to restore faith in the herd."

"A grisly way to restore faith that's bringing them the type of attention they don't want."

"Unless they spin it," Willa said with a look of disgust. "Think about it. Every time something horrible happens in this town, their numbers only grow."

There was no denying that was true. "It could also be someone with a grievance against the Shining Light. You saw those protesters. Half of this town has been aching to get rid of them for years. Don't forget the reason we need to speak with Arlo tomorrow. If it's true Empyrean has been blackmailing former members, people have killed for far less."

"Gemma didn't have a tattoo. How did the killer know Gemma had spent time among them unless he was one of them? The compound, the rules, the lack of a vehicle, the vows to the Light, it's all the perfect cover for a killer. I guarantee you not everyone who joins gives up all their possessions. Easy enough to stash a car not far away. Use an account that he didn't turn over to Empyrean to pay for the gas. It's feasible."

Daniel nodded. "It is." He pulled down the blinds to his window overlooking the bullpen and closed them. He did the same for the ones over the glass door and leaned against it. "Did your son give up everything when he joined?"

Willa's stomach soured. This was coming, she'd been aware, but it didn't make her any more ready to have the conversation. Setting her feet down on the floor, she stood and folded her arms. "He didn't have much to give up. He ran away from home and joined when he was seventeen."

"Why did he leave?"

"Ever since his father, my ex-husband, Zach, was killed in the line of duty, he was never the same." She should've taken him to grief counseling. His grandmother had mocked the idea, putting it into his head that only the weak cried to a therapist. Still, she should've dragged him anyway. Explained that getting help was a sign of strength. "He ended up on the compound.

Zeke told McCoy I was a cop. That combined with his age was the only reason I received a phone call, letting me know he was there before I put out an APB on him."

"Why did you let him stay?"

"McCoy talked to me. The man is very good at what he does. Charming. Convincing. It was the end of the school year. Zeke was already failing his classes and had been expelled for fighting. McCoy persuaded me to let him explore the community over the summer. To see if it made a difference in him. I was desperate. All I wanted was for him to get better."

"And he did?"

She nodded. "He was like a different person. Happy. Smiling. Laughing." It had brought her tears of joy to see him that way. "They had even worked with him on his studies. Helped him to get his GED over the summer. He told me he wanted to stay because he'd found the Light. McCoy warned me that if he left, he'd fall back into darkness. He tapped into my greatest fear."

"Of course, you supported him staying."

How could she not? "After he took his vows and became a Starlight, he didn't want to see me or his grandmother. He claimed everything he needed was there on the compound with his new family." The words had been like a hot knife in the heart. "That was my baby. I loved him so much, but I let him go." Every parent had to at some point. She learned to love at a distance, relinquish her expectations and embrace his choices. "Until he came back to me a few years later after he was kicked out."

"For what?"

"I don't know. You have no idea how tempted I was to be the one to get the files."

"What does he say when you ask him?"

"To leave it alone. Then he clams up and storms out or shouts and storms out. Either way, I, the chief of police, can't get a straight answer out of my own son." Saying it aloud only made her even more disgusted and disappointed with herself.

Daniel crossed the room and clasped her shoulders. "You're being too hard on yourself."

Was she? "I'm failing him. I'm so afraid I might lose him if I don't figure out how to fix whatever is wrong. I should be able to do more, but I feel...helpless when it comes to him."

He pulled her into a gentle hug. She wanted to relax into it, but part of her didn't deserve comfort for not doing a good enough job with her kid.

"You're more than a cop. You're a single mother doing the best you can." With one arm around her, he rubbed her back with the other.

"I was raised by a single mother. My dad died when I was twelve."

The same age as Zeke. Was it a sign all hope wasn't lost?

"I had some troubled years. My mother threw money at the problem, thinking her wealth was the solution," he said, his voice warm and soothing as a shot of whiskey, and she leaned against him. "Don't get me wrong, when I got kicked out of one private school, she bought my way into another. But it wasn't until I left home, stopped blaming her for everything that was wrong in my life, claimed my inheritance, my father's ranch out here, that I was able to fix it for myself. Then I became a cop."

"You grew up with a silver spoon in your mouth?"

He chuckled, the smooth sound vibrating through her. "After everything I told you, that's your takeaway?"

She gave him a sad smile. "It distracted me."

"Well, if you need a distraction, I can do better. My mother is Selene Beauvais."

Surprise slid through her. "No way." She'd never been the type to buy fashion magazines or read about runway shows featuring couture, but she would have to live under a rock not to have heard of the legendary supermodel Selene Beauvais.

He hitched up a shoulder. "Way." He stroked her hair, his fingers feathering her ear and her gaze dropped to his mouth.

She missed kissing him, lying in bed, snuggled close. Even if it had only lasted a few months. He'd made an impression that she couldn't forget.

"The point I want you to remember is single mothers are heroes, but superheroes don't exist. Cut yourself some slack. You can't do the work for him."

Everything he said made perfect sense in her head. She just needed her heart to accept the logic. "You're right. Thanks for the support."

"I'd like to support you more. But for some reason you simply cut me off. Can I know why?"

She dropped her arms, ending the embrace, but stayed close to him. Absorbing the smell of him. His warmth. His quiet strength.

"You have no idea how hard it's been for me. Not only as a single mother. But to climb the ranks in the police force and become the first female chief of two different departments."

"Yeah. How would I, the first Black sheriff of Albany County, have any idea what you might be going through professionally. When

I first got this job, it wasn't through an election. I was appointed because the last sheriff had made such a mess of things and caused a scandal. It wasn't until I faced an opponent and became elected by the people that my critics started to treat me differently."

Once again, he was right. They had much more in common than she had realized. "We were lovers, but we had also been friends. Sort of." On the verge of becoming such. "I'm sorry I never stopped to consider what you were facing. But it's different for me. As a woman people make assumptions about how I got here. If they knew we had been seeing each other at the time it only would've fed into the narrow-minded notion that I had somehow slept my way to the top even though the mayor appointed me."

He nodded. "But that was then. We've kept our distance, and both proven ourselves for the last two years. Why can't there be an us now?"

A knock at the door had them separating by a good two feet.

Willa was grateful for the interruption. She needed time to think. Her first response would have been that the job was too demanding, requiring all her time and effort. But the truth was the biggest hurdle of cleaning up the department was behind her. Now it was about replenishing her ranks with good police officers and catching a serial killer. Beyond that, Daniel faced the same demands as her and if anyone would understand and accommodate without complaint, it was him.

"Enter," he said, his gaze lingering on her like a soft caress until the door opened.

Deputy Russo came in. "I read the transcripts of the unburdening sessions that McCoy conducted right before they took their vows. The women had been given ayahuasca, a drug they use in their religious ceremonies."

"You're saying they were high when they unburdened," Daniel said.

"Precisely. Nothing noteworthy came up with Gooding. Jealousy of her friends who had cute boyfriends, enough money for college and a sense of purpose. It was the last one that McCoy focused on with her."

Willa put a little more distance between her and Daniel. "And Fisher?"

"She had a history of prostitution and stealing because she was struggling with substance abuse."

"And he dosed her with ayahuasca?" Daniel asked.

Russo nodded. "According to the document that detailed why she left, the ayahuasca triggered cravings that had gone away. It was difficult for her to stay clean again. She broke into the infirmary twice and offered sexual favors to the security team if they would get her something, anything to get high. McCoy couldn't help her. So, when they kicked her out, McCoy had her dropped off at a church that holds NA meetings."

"Unbelievable." Daniel folded his arms. "McCoy got her clean only to mess her up all over again."

"He's playing God on that compound. It's shameful." Willa shook her head. "What was the situation behind Gooding leaving?"

Russo's mouth twisted. "Not quite sure. It stated that she was *allowed* to leave to attend college for a year. It would appease her parents and facilitate a smooth transition if she decided to return. But she would be considered one of the Fallen until the day," she said, pausing as she looked at her notepad, "and I quote, 'The Light spoke to Empyrean guiding him to do otherwise with the sweet child Lila,' end quote."

"He created a loophole," Willa said. "One to allow her to come back and for him to cash her parents' check. No mention of money by any chance?"

"Nope. Sorry." Russo frowned. "The ME

won't be able to start on the body for a few hours. Family emergency."

"Okay," Daniel said. "Go to the church— see what they have to say about Fisher. Also question the employees at the bus station. See if they saw or heard anything strange or out of the ordinary."

"I'll head over there now." Russo left the office as Livingston entered.

"Statements from Gemma Chavez's parents and her best friend," the deputy said. "I'm still trying to get in contact with other friends her parents mentioned."

Daniel took the folder. The phone on his desk beeped. He put it on speaker and answered, "What is it, Peggy?"

"District Attorney Jennings and Mayor Schroeder request your and Chief Nelson's presence at the mayor's office over at city hall. Right now."

Daniel groaned. "All right." He hung up. "One guess what the topic of conversation will be," he said, sarcastically.

This case and three dead women. Willa met Daniel's gaze. "Right about now, I'm glad you suggested we work together on this one."

"Why? So we can share the heat?"

She smiled even though they were about to walk into the fire. "Exactly."

"Then I think you owe me one. How about you buy me a drink?"

"Just a drink?" she asked, knowing better.

A deep chuckle rumbled in his chest. "Well…let's play it by ear."

The sound of his laughter and the suggestion of one drink dragged her back to their first meeting at Crazy Eddie's. The bar was a dive outside of Wayward Bluffs before you reached Laramie, in the middle of nowhere. A place for truckers and ranch hands. She'd never worn makeup or a smile and didn't accept drinks someone else had purchased. Her reputation for being the tough woman no one bothered had been hard-earned until Daniel had waltzed in and had the guts to claim the stool beside her.

With a scowl, her brush-off had been, "Cowboy, no offense, but *I* don't want company and if *you* don't want trouble, you'll take a hike."

Still, that hadn't discouraged him. "Depends on the kind of trouble."

She'd pointed to her Wayward Bluffs badge on her hip that had sent most men skittering. "I'm Chief Nelson, so we're talking police trouble. Still interested?"

He had simply flashed his own badge from the SWU campus police. "Nice to meet you,

I'm Chief Clark, but I'd prefer it if you called me Daniel."

She had been a goner right there, but something in her wouldn't let her buckle. The more she'd played hard to get over the weeks that had followed, the more interested he'd seemed. One night, she'd taken the time to explain her reasons why a relationship of any kind was out of the question. Though she was single, she had a complicated family—leaving it open to interpretation—and a job that demanded all her energy. A man in her life would have required time and effort she didn't want to give.

"I've picked two duds before, which is proof that dating isn't for me," she had confided, breaking her rules and engaging in conversation with him every time he'd walked into that bar.

"Maybe the third time is the charm."

She'd given him more honesty. "I don't have that kind of luck."

"I do." Another irresistible smile that made her thighs tingle. "I've got enough for both of us."

Unsure what exactly it had been, his infectious confidence, his calm demeanor, his easy way with her or that he'd simply worn her down, she'd suggested that they get a room at the motel down the road. Eventually, the motel had turned into nights at his place.

Then she'd gotten the job in the LPD and had ended it.

"Hey." Daniel waved in front of her face, bringing her back to the here and now. "What do you say?"

"It's never just a drink, cowboy."

He gave her another slow grin that sent a zing of anticipation jolting through her, and she smiled in return. "No, Willa, I guess not." His chuckle was low and knowing. "I suppose when it comes to you, it's always more than just a drink."

Conversation. Lovemaking. Snuggling. Showers together. Sometimes even breakfast, too.

Her body ached for all of it. She'd gone two years without being touched. Not even a hug from her son. But her head told her to slow down. Not to throw caution to the wind without thinking it through first.

"Let's talk after we deal with the mayor and the DA."

Chapter Six

"Good evening, Mayor Schroeder, DA Jennings," Daniel said, taking off his hat.

"What can we do for you?" Willa asked.

Sitting behind his oversized mahogany desk, the mayor glanced at the DA, who stood beside him, red-faced and clearly steaming.

"I'm going to cut right to it," Allen Jennings said. "You two came to me, requesting assistance on a quick turnaround warrant, and I was more than happy to oblige. You went to the compound, questioned a suspect and released him. We have three dead women. Three! Why wasn't he charged?"

Word spread fast, which meant Daniel had someone in his office leaking information to the DA's office. But that was an issue for another time. More pressing was that if Daniel knew anything about Willa, it was that she would not abide anyone talking to her that way.

While he on the other hand had perfected

the art of not letting it get to him. Well, not letting it show anyway.

Before he could get a word out, she opened her mouth first.

"He had an alibi and we had no evidence." Willa put her hands on her hips. "Simple as that. It's called adhering to the law."

Narrowing his eyes, Jennings marched around the desk. "Don't presume to dictate to me about the law."

"We're all on the same side, working toward a common goal." Daniel stepped in between them. "I think we need to bring the temperature down a couple of degrees and let cooler heads prevail."

"McCoy is behind this." For a small wiry man with a thick shock of white hair and a penchant for bow ties, Jennings had a big presence that filled a room and a voice that belonged to a man twice his size. "What is it going to take for you two to do your job and bring me something I can convict him on?"

"I'm inclined to agree with Chief Nelson," Daniel said. "Evidence."

"Then find some, damn it. Every day that menace of a man plays the pied piper, stealing more children, brainwashing wives, corrupting husbands and sucking up souls like the devil on earth with a spiritual vacuum cleaner is a day that you," Jennings said, pointing at Willa, "and you—" his finger swung to Daniel "—have failed to do your jobs and handicapped me from doing mine!"

Whoa. To Daniel this almost felt personal. Jennings's comment about stealing children must've struck a nerve with Willa because she didn't respond. Daniel looked to the mayor to gauge where he stood on this.

Schroeder's face was solemn, but he remained quiet, which told Daniel that Jennings had gone running to the mayor and made a fuss.

"We're doing everything we can to stop a killer," Daniel clarified. "That may or may not give you McCoy." He doubted that it would.

"I was so close. This close," Jennings said, holding up to two fingers separated by a mere inch, "to getting the Shining Light and that sanctimonious Marshall McCoy on tax fraud charges, then my witness got scared and went quiet on me before handing over evidence. The next thing I know his cult somehow managed to get tax-exemption status like pulling a bunny out of a hat."

"Who is your witness?" Willa asked.

Jennings finally shut up, his gaze bouncing between them.

Daniel sighed. "You can't drag us in here,

berate us and not trust us enough to put your cards on the table and tell us the truth. We need to share information."

"He's right," the mayor said. "Tell them."

Jennings scrubbed a hand over his face as he considered it. "Arlo Starlight. She won't talk to me anymore. I think she's worried that the evidence will be traced back to her."

Willa looked at him, the question gleamed clear in her eyes. He gave a curt, subtle nod. After all, he was the one advocating disclosure in the spirit of cooperation.

"Mercy McCoy told us that her father uses the unburdening tapes," Willa said, "where members share compromising information, against them."

Jennings jumped on that. "Against them how?"

Daniel shook his head. "We don't know. But we plan to find out."

"When?" the mayor and Jennings asked in unison.

"Tomorrow," Daniel said. "If we learn anything, we'll let you know." The last thing he wanted was to be a hypocrite by withholding information, but Mercy had trusted them to approach Arlo about this in a sensitive manner. Honestly, Daniel had serious doubts regarding Jennings's ability to be sensitive.

"Listen, I'm going to give it to you straight," Mayor Schroeder said, "we have protesters outside the Shining Light's compound. Once the news breaks about the third body, the numbers are going to triple. I don't want this city turning into a tinderbox. Your top priority should be to find this killer and put him behind bars. Secondary is solving the problem of the cult. We all suspect illegal activity is happening on the compound. Thus far, we've been unable to get anything on Marshall McCoy. And that's after I brought in a joint task force to focus on them." He put an elbow on his desk and rubbed his brow. "Willa, you did an outstanding job clearing the debris out of the department. But I need more from you. I'm planning on running for governor and on that same ticket will be Allen for attorney general. We need this Starlight Killer caught. And McCoy. Or I'll have to appoint someone else who can do it."

She rocked back on her heels. "Are you threatening my job?"

Schroeder shook his head. "I don't threaten. I inform. I incentivize. Your son is no longer a member of the Shining Light, but it's my understanding that he's having difficulty reacclimating," he said, and Willa suddenly looked worried as if surprised he had that information. "Allen's daughter is a Starlight, spinning in circles and dancing under the moon. You both have skin in the game. You just need a little extra motivation." His gaze shifted. "Daniel, where do you stand regarding the Shining Light?"

"I stand on the side of the law. If McCoy is guilty of something and we can nail him, we will. But my job doesn't solely cover their compound. I'm responsible for all of Albany County and my duty is to the citizens who elected me. Regarding the serial killer, we may be dealing with a copycat. Someone murdering women in the same manner as the Holiday Elk Horn Killer."

"Your office mishandled that case," Jennings said full of vitriol, as though Daniel had been the sheriff five years ago. "It would behoove you to ensure your department doesn't let a cold-blooded murderer get away a second time, especially if he's a member of the Shining Light."

The DA was practically foaming at the mouth with hatred for McCoy. Now knowing that Jennings had skin in the game—a daughter who had become a Starlight—he couldn't help but wonder how far the district attorney, a father, would go to tear down the Shining Light.

"If this tinderbox ignites," Mayor Schroeder

said, "it will be the problem of everyone in this room. Do not let that happen. Not on my watch."

A riot in town, or worse, an attack against the compound, wouldn't look good on the mayor's résumé in his bid for governor. But Daniel had hoped the man's primary concern would have been the protection of the citizens, not safeguarding his political future.

"I can assure you we will do everything in our power to keep that from happening," Daniel said.

Schroeder leaned back in his chair. "See that you do. Both of you." He fixed his gaze on Willa. "Because if this turns into an unmitigated disaster, the fallout won't land on this office," the mayor said, reaffirming his intent to place the blame on the chief of police.

In the corridor, on their way down the hall, Daniel said, "If this doesn't shake out the way we'd like, don't worry, I won't let the mayor railroad you out of your job."

"And how precisely would you stop him?"

"I'd hold a press conference. Tell everyone that I took over the case from you and accept full responsibility for any failure. Then I would sing your praises about how your office did everything possible to assist. If he tried to fire you after that, it would come across loud and clear to the public for what it was. A politician trying to cover his own behind."

She put a hand on his shoulder, stopping him. A look he couldn't quite decipher came over her face. "Why would you do that for me?"

He cared about her, and she did not deserve to get fired to advance the political career of a selfish coward. "You're an excellent chief. You accomplished something in your department that your predecessors couldn't. And I don't like bullies. We work damn hard, risking our lives for this job. We shouldn't be treated as pawns." Schroeder rubbed him the wrong way, and now Daniel would do what he could to protect Willa.

She stared at him for several heartbeats, and he wished he could read her thoughts. "We didn't get a chance to eat lunch earlier and now it's time for dinner. How about we leave the delivery order in the fridge for tomorrow and you come back to my house?"

He grinned, happy for the invitation. The possibilities of where the night might lead ignited a fire in his bloodstream. He remembered every inch of her body, long and trim, athletic and strong. Full breasts. Sinewy legs. Every time they'd slept together, he had reveled in the feel and taste of her, drawing out every sensual moment, savoring the bittersweet sensation, like that experience might be his last with her. But their first night, after weeks of flirting— and it had been a while for him—he'd needed her so much he'd been a wild man. Looking at her now still triggered that gut-aching desire.

Not love, but more than like, his affection for her combined with his sexual impulses created one heck of a reaction in his body.

"I mean for work," she clarified, dampening his excitement. "We can make a quick bite to eat, review the Chavez statements, cross-reference the lists of members against those of the recent Fallen and wait for the autopsy report," she said, listing the mountain of work they had to do.

During their fling, they had not gone back to her place a single time. At first, he'd simply been thrilled about the upgrade from the impersonal motel to his house. Then he'd figured that she had needed the convenience and ease of leaving when she wanted, avoiding the awkwardness and hassle of asking him to go. But after she had cut off all communication without explanation and stopped showing up at Crazy Eddie's, he'd realized she had never wanted him to know her phone number, much less where she lived.

It wasn't as if he would have gone looking

for her at her job, which struck him as borderline stalkerish. His mother had raised him to be a gentleman and he had the common sense to take a hint.

"A working dinner sounds good to me." Since they weren't eating in the office, he wanted to take this as a sign that she was willing to trust him even if it didn't mean more than that.

"I have to warn you, my place is small," she said. "Actually, it's a tiny cabin in a remote area. But if Wayward Bluffs is too far for you to drive, then we could do dinner at your place."

There was no way on earth he was turning her down. If he did, he might not get a second chance. "Your place is perfect."

DANIEL STOOD IN Willa's cramped kitchen, chopping vegetables like a proper sous chef. "This was a great idea," he said, and she spotted a flicker of desire in his eyes.

"Yeah." Willa hoped she didn't come to regret it. She'd never brought him here before in an effort to keep their dalliance from blossoming into something more. She hadn't worried he would have shown up unannounced. Pointing a loaded shotgun at a person had a way of dissuading a guy from returning without an invitation. It was just that once she opened her life to someone, invited them in, it was hard to close that door.

Maybe Daniel was right. They'd both proven themselves. He'd won his election. She'd been praised by the mayor and the media for cleaning up a dirty department—an accomplishment no one could take away from her. If they could stop this serial killer and nail McCoy, she'd have no qualms about exploring the possibility of a relationship.

Daniel got her. Her need for space and discretion. The hardship of being a single mother. And no one else would understand better than he did the commitment and sacrifices this job demanded.

Not only did she respect him, but she felt safe with him, trusted him and desired him in a way that she had never experienced before. She'd been attracted to him from his opening lines in Crazy Eddie's, and she knew she'd never tire of appreciating him physically ever since watching him build a fire at his place one night when his shirt had lifted, exposing bare skin. But she stayed careful. Cautious.

Less so now that she was aware what he was willing to risk for her. He treated her as more of a partner on this case than the man she'd foolishly and reluctantly married. She was amazed that he was willing to jeopardize his position as sheriff to save her job.

No one had ever been on her side in that way.

"Add the veggies to the sauce," she said.

He dumped the chopped zucchini, spinach, kale and mushrooms in. Leaning close, he watched her stir the pot of quick homemade marinara. She flicked a glance at his handsome face, letting her gaze slide to his broad chest, the ripples of muscle straining against his shirt. A little thrill whipped through her. A memory came rushing back, of how it felt to run her fingers over his bare skin, the masculine sound of pleasure he made when she pressed her lips to his—

Nope. Going there would only mean trouble.

The timer beeped, refocusing her. "Mind draining the rotini?" She already had a colander in the sink.

"Sure." He slid around behind her, his body grazing hers in the narrow galley kitchen, and grabbed the pot.

"Save a little of the water to add to the sauce along with the pasta."

"That's a trick I use myself. My mother's chef taught me."

She still found it hard to believe that his mother was rich and famous and one of the most beautiful women in the world. Now she knew where he got his good looks from—and he was hot. "Must have been nice growing up with all that wealth."

He poured a quarter cup of water into the sauce and then added the pasta, and she went back to stirring, giving the rotini a chance to absorb the flavors.

"Not really. She wasn't around too much when I was younger, always jet-setting off for work or fun. The privileged lifestyle catered to her—not to kids. But when you grow up with a silver spoon in your mouth as you say, you can't complain."

"Sure, you had safety, shelter, private schools, a chef, probably tutors," she said, and he nodded, "and never wanted for any material thing, but that doesn't replace a mother's presence. Trust me, I know. My son reminds me every chance he gets that all his life I've put my career first, with the long hours and overtime. Then as a cop you have to separate the horror and awful stuff that desensitizes you over time from your home life and there are moments when you're so drained, you're a shell of person, going through the motions. Giving as much as you can, but it's never enough."

She took a deep breath, not knowing where all of that had come from. But it felt good to say it, to get it out. That was the effect he had on her. Got her to lower her guard and talk.

With a sympathetic look, he put a hand to her back and rubbed. "Even though I've never been married and don't have kids, I get it. A few months before we met, my girlfriend of three years dumped me." He met her gaze and must've seen the questions in her eyes. "For all the reasons you mentioned. I didn't want to bring the darkness home, didn't want to talk about it and she felt shut out. The hours and the emergencies were too much for her. On campus we were understaffed, and you wouldn't believe the number of incidents that occurred. She eventually accepted a job in Omaha. Not long after I started as sheriff, she asked me to visit to be sure our breakup wasn't a mistake."

She started plating the food. "I guess it wasn't."

"After being with you I knew it wasn't because I had stopped missing her. Then when I got there, she wanted me to change career fields and move to Nebraska. Become a real estate agent of all things. Can you imagine?"

They both laughed.

She handed him a plate and grabbed a bottle of wine. "One glass with dinner?"

"You do owe me a drink."

They went to the table and sat. She put a

small dish of grated Parmesan cheese down. He sprinkled a healthy amount over his pasta as she poured the wine.

"Sonia didn't understand that this job is a calling." He dug into the food and gave a satisfied moan. "This is excellent."

In high school, she'd known a Sonia—a selfish, mean girl. "Being a cop gets in your blood. Becomes a part of you that you can't shut off." She took a mouthful as well, pleased she done a good job with limited ingredients and in a hurry.

"Exactly," he said with a nod. "What made you want to become a police officer?"

"My dad was a cop. My ex, too. Zach joined the force a year before we separated. After the divorce, I had been working two jobs to make ends meet on my own, in an effort to show my father that I would never be anything like him because he was an alcoholic, verbally abusive, distant tyrant who wanted me to be a cop. Anyway, I had started entertaining the idea of accepting my boss's invitation to go out on a date. He promoted me to assistant manager at the grocery store. One night, we were the only ones there and he thought I should be nicer to him."

"As in sleep with him nicer?"

"You've got it. A conversation turned

heated, there was grabbing and then hitting and the next thing I knew I was fighting for my life. I hit him with something hard and knocked him out cold. Called the police. And I had never been so happy to see a couple of uniforms show up. He came to and when they put him in cuffs and shoved him into the back of a cruiser, I wished that had been me. Cuffing him and taking him to the precinct. I applied the next day."

"You're a fighter. A survivor. You didn't let him steal your peace of mind or your power."

She took a sip of wine. "You?"

"I worked on a ranch when I moved out here. The owner turned out to have been an old friend of my father's. During those long, hard days I learned what it meant to be a cowboy, from understanding the grass cycles to timing the calving season to maximize those cycles, bull genetics and diseases. It wasn't easy."

"If it was easy, everyone would be a cowboy."

A hint of a smile tugged at his mouth. "Anyway cattle kept going missing. The owner would file reports with the local brand inspector, the Livestock Board, the sheriff. Nothing. I investigated on my own. Found the culprit. In the process of bringing him to justice, I took two to the chest."

She'd seen the gunshot wounds and had asked. All he had said was it had been the price for getting justice for a friend.

"Anyway, I ended up becoming a criminal investigator for the Livestock Board. I loved wearing the badge and solving cases, but there was no room to grow. An opening with the campus police popped up right when I was looking for a change. I took it and worked up the ranks fast."

"Nearly dying didn't scare you off. Because you're a fighter, too."

"Guess we're two peas in a pod." He slid her a sexy look that sent a flutter through her belly.

The room shrank around them, becoming more cozy, more intimate.

"I guess so." Averting her gaze, she struggled and failed to shake off the sensation.

She shoved more food in her mouth before she said something provocative. Around him she felt sexy and seen and she didn't intimidate him. He took her in stride. Her suggestive comments seemed to stoke a fire in him and when they came together they both burned.

Less talking. More eating. And get to work.

She glanced up and found his gaze on her. "Why are you staring? Do I have something on my face?" She touched the corner of her mouth.

"A bit of sauce." He reached over, wiped the opposite side, and sucked it from his finger.

She squeezed her thighs together at the way he made the simplest action sexy.

"But you are awfully hard not to notice," he said with a devilish grin.

Her face heated, and she cleared her throat. "Which folder do you want? Chavez statements or cross-referencing the cult's lists?" she asked, pointing to the folders she'd left on the counter.

"The lady gets to choose." There was a flirtatious twinkle in his eyes.

"I never said I was a lady." She was treading into dangerous territory, but the words had left her mouth without thinking.

One of his brows quirked. "You're certainly not in the bedroom. Part cougar I think from the way you pounce and the marks you leave on my back." He let out a low chuckle as his gaze skated down her body.

She tingled all over. "Flip you for it."

"Are we talking a coin, or do you want to wrestle again?"

The wrestling match in the motel room had been a result of too much whiskey and her trying to prove she could take him. She had too, pinning him quickly. Until he'd shoved his pelvis up, flipped her over, and became the one on top with her happy to be trapped beneath him. Then they had stripped each other in a mad rush, kissing and tasting. Lips running over bare skin. Arms tangling. His hips urging her legs to part.

"On second thought, I'll just take the lists." She stood.

So did he, sidestepping to block her. She could have easily walked around him if she'd wanted, but she didn't move. She barely breathed.

Standing in front of each other, toe to toe, he gripped her chin between two fingers and tilted her face up a fraction, meeting her gaze. "The one thing we've both learned is that life is short. We have to make the most of the time we have."

Not suppressing the primal urge, she did.

She wrapped her arms around his neck, pulling his mouth to hers, and kissed him with all the pent-up emotion begging for release. He kissed her back, hot and hungry. She wanted him. Body and soul. And she didn't care about tomorrow or the consequences. She wasn't going to let this moment slip away from her.

He groaned as his arms tightened around her, one warm hand pressed to her spine and the other cupped her backside, pulling her closer. There was an urgency in his touch, in his kisses.

Her lower belly heated, desire spreading through her, rushing in her veins, pounding in her ears. It had been so long since she'd been held, touched like this, and never had she been so impatient, her body rousing with each sensation he made flare.

A car door slammed closed outside.

Her eyes flew open, gaze going to the window. Footsteps stomped up the porch. Keys jangled.

Sighing at the awful timing, she let Daniel go and hurriedly fixed her appearance, smoothing her hair, hoping the flush was gone from her cheeks.

The knob turned. The door opened.

Zeke stepped inside, slamming the door closed and stopped short. "Who in the hell is this?"

"Hello to you, too," she said, straining for calm and patience. "This is Sheriff Daniel Clark."

Her son grimaced, his gaze taking in the room. "I can't believe you're dating a cop. You'd think you'd have the common sense to find somebody with a profession *less* dangerous and *less* stressful than yours."

"We're not dating." Her cheeks heated. "We're working a case together."

Zeke rolled his eyes. "Yeah, okay. I'm going to grab some food, go to my room and you two can get back to wining and dining. I mean 'working,'" he said using air quotes.

Embarrassment was like a red-hot poker in her gut. "For your information this is a working dinner."

"Whatever." He stormed past her into the kitchen and peered into the pot. "Is this vegetarian?"

"Yes." She'd gotten into the habit of making meatless meals in an effort to help him with his transition. "What are you doing here? I thought you were staying at your grandmother's," she said, flicking a glance at Daniel.

He sat down and went back to eating.

"She got upset with me, so I bounced. I'm going to crash here for a bit. They changed me to the graveyard shift over at the gas station. I've got to be there at two a.m. Can you believe they told me at the last minute and expect me to show up?"

"Yes, it's a called a job. You had yesterday off." Willa went up to him in the kitchen and put a hand on his shoulder. "Why is your grandmother upset?"

He must've seriously messed up if the older

woman wasn't happy with the boy-who-did-no-wrong.

Zeke jerked away from her touch. "It's my business with Grandma." He ladled a mound of pasta into a deep bowl. "You don't want me up in your business, right? Or would you rather I eat at the table and get an up-close look at you in action. *Working.* Don't you usually go over cases in an office?"

Shutting her eyes for a moment, she drew in a deep breath. How had it gotten this bad? Had it happened slowly or in a great horrendous slide like an avalanche, burying her.

"You won't speak to me that way." She fixed him with a stare. "Not in my house."

Zeke put his hand up to his mouth, motioning like he was inserting a key and turning a lock. Spinning on his heel, he strode to the table, put Parmesan on his food, gave Daniel a two-finger salute and stormed off to his room, slamming the door closed. A second later the television came on.

Willa was mortified. She could melt into the floor. "I'm so sorry—"

"Why are you sorry?" Another sympathetic look. "He's the one who should be apologizing."

"But I'm the one who lets him get away with

it." If she scolded him, putting her foot down, she'd only drive him away.

At least she knew he was safe, warm and well-fed while under her roof.

Daniel got up, came over to her, and clutched her shoulders. His steel grip steadied her from the outside in. "It's complicated. You two have been through a lot together. Add in the Machiavellian factor of the cult and who is to judge? Certainly not me. Cut yourself some..."

"Slack?" Easier said than done.

He grabbed the folders from the counter and handed her one. "Let's show him what *work* looks like. Besides, we have to be up at the crack of dawn in order to catch Arlo in the morning."

He turned to go to the table, and she caught his hand.

"Thank you."

"For what?"

Being so incredible. "Understanding. Not judging." And if he was, he kept it to himself, thankfully. "Making me feel better." A miracle in itself.

"That's what partners do. Good ones anyway."

She'd been saddled with lousy ones for sure, but she wondered if he was only talking about work and them on this case.

Sitting down and opening the folder, she decided it didn't matter. For as long as he was her partner, whether it was a day, a week, or longer, she wouldn't take it for granted.

Chapter Seven

Picking up his coffee from the cup holder in the SUV, Daniel took a sip. At the early hour, with the sun barely up, his body needed the caffeine, but his restless mind kept churning over the case. According to Gemma's best friend, she'd left home because her stepdad had been handsy. After bouncing between jobs, with no stable place to live, sleeping on her best friend's couch, she'd picked up a flyer for the Shining Light. Her friend had gotten a boyfriend. Gemma hadn't wanted to overstay her welcome. The compound was a good alternative until they had a lockdown after receiving a threat that terrorists might attack the commune. That combined with Mercy leaving the community was a sign that she should go, too.

"I can't stop thinking about the Chavez statements," Daniel said to Willa.

"You doubt the veracity?" she asked from the passenger seat.

"No. I buy the reasons for her turning to the cult. I even believe what McCoy told us, that the lockdown and his heir apparent, Mercy, choosing to become one of the Fallen was enough to send her running for the hills. Miguel dropped her off a week ago. Surveillance footage at the bus station shows it. Then she doesn't visit her parents or her best friend and simply disappears until we found her dead body yesterday?"

"Do you think the mother, or the girlfriend is lying? The stepdad took her, killed her? But what about the other two?"

"I'm not saying they're lying. I'm saying that it's strange for her to disappear." He took another sip of the strong, hot brew. "What if the killer grabbed her and held her for a week waiting for the full moon?"

"No defensive wounds," she said, referring to the autopsy report that had come in late last night. "Pretty hard to hold a woman against her will without her getting some. I suppose he could've drugged her, but nothing was found in her system. It would've been tedious to use chloroform for that long."

"He could've dosed her with something for several days. Then used chloroform short-term, giving the other drug time to leave her system and we wouldn't pick it up."

"Either way, it supports your theory that the killer is someone on the outside." She took a gulp of her coffee. "I was really hoping that cross-referencing the two lists would have given us something. I thought for sure a member who had joined four to five years ago, right after the Holiday Elk Horn Murders stopped, would have been on the list of the Fallen, who had been cast out or had decided to break their vows this year."

"We do have something. A list of potential suspects to question." Once Livingston got into the office, he would start working on tracking them all down. Four individuals, one being Ezekiel Nelson. They had to question him, surely Willa was aware of that, but Daniel had yet to discuss it with her.

The white van with the Shining Light symbol on the side came around the corner, headed down the road in their direction, where they weren't easily visible behind a sign.

Mercy had told them which route to take. On this particular stretch of road, it was easy to exceed the speed limit unless the driver was a stickler for watching the gauge.

They were hoping to get lucky.

Willa held up the velocity speed gun, aimed and pulled the trigger. The van passed. A smile spread across her face, and she turned to display the screen to him.

There was nothing complicated about how Wyoming's absolute speed limits worked. If you drove faster than the posted speed, you'd violated the law. In this case, the driver was going thirty-six in a thirty-mph zone.

Daniel hit his lights, not bothering with the siren.

It took the driver less than a minute to respond, stopping on the side of the road.

Daniel pulled up behind them and they both got out, approaching the driver's side.

Miguel was behind the wheel and rolled down the window. He looked crestfallen to see them. "Hi, Sheriff, Chief Nelson. Is there a problem?"

"You were speeding," Willa said with a stern face. "Six miles over the limit."

"Oh, I'm so sorry. I didn't realize it."

"Who's in charge of this outing?" Daniel looked over the passengers, his gaze settling on the woman with glasses and a gray bob.

"I am."

"Ma'am, can you step out of the vehicle." Daniel walked around to the passenger side as Willa resumed going through the motions with Miguel.

The sliding door whooshed open, and Arlo

climbed out. "My apologies for exceeding the speed limit. Fox is usually such a careful driver."

"Please close the door and follow me."

Her face twisted in confusion. She slid the door shut and trailed behind to the SUV.

He stopped in front of his vehicle, keeping his back to it where he could keep an eye on the rear of the van and track how Willa was doing.

"What's going on, Sheriff?"

"State your name for me," he said, double-checking he had the right person.

"Arlo Starlight. We have all the proper documentation. Fox's license is current."

"Mercy thought you might help us," he said, with no time to ease into it.

Her eyes fluttered with surprise "Help with what?" She was about to look over her shoulder.

"Don't turn around. Stay focused on me," he said, and she did. "We know you were working with DA Jennings to get him evidence of tax evasion."

"I can't help with that." She shook her head, her expression grim. "If I provide documentation, it will trace back to me."

"Has McCoy used information from unburdening sessions to blackmail or extort present or former members?"

She stood still and silent, her gaze not wavering as she deliberated how to respond.

Daniel frowned, watching Willa review the documentation that Miguel handed her. "We don't have much time."

Finally, she nodded.

"How did he use it against them? Was it to get the tax-exemption status as a religious organization?"

More deliberation.

Willa glanced at him, checking in.

He shook his head, indicating he needed more time. "Please," he said to Arlo.

"The entire commune will suffer if the tax-exemption status is revoked," she said. "With the amount of back taxes, we might lose the land. We'd all be homeless with nowhere to go."

Miguel got out of the van and Willa started giving him a field sobriety test.

Daniel took out his notepad. "Mercy said to tell you that she left because her father is the devil. A liar. *Evil.* His darkness has tainted everything he's built and will one day be destroyed because of his wickedness."

Arlo hunched over, clutching her chest like the words had sent her into cardiac arrest.

"You must have your doubts about him, too," Daniel said.

Another nod.

"Give me names of the people he black-mailed."

She sucked in a strained breath. He could only imagine how her faith must have been rocked to the core.

"Not about the taxes," she said, her voice shaky. "The rest of us have too much to lose. We do such good work. Save so many lives. Marshall is corrupt. We must cut him out as a doctor would a cancerous tumor. I have believed this for a long time. But I won't endanger the commune."

"I don't want five hundred people to suffer because of the wrongdoings of one man. You must know something that I can give to the DA so he can go after him. Just him."

A tear leaked from the corner of her eye, and she whisked it away. "Roger Hines," she said, and he started writing. "Elmer Clayborne and Felicia Pietsch."

"Councilwoman Pietsch?"

A slow, grave nod. "Marshall extorted them for money."

"Are you sure?"

"I was there when he approached the councilwoman at her home back in June. He alluded to her husband's unburdening session. She played dumb. He asked me to leave the room. We left with a check for seventy-five thousand dollars. Marshall and I fought over it. He dismissed my opinion and commanded me to silence. Two more checks came in following his visits to the others. A quarter million in total. He used it to buy us time with the taxes until he could finagle our status as a religious organization."

The sum was shocking. "Do you know what he had on them?"

"Not all of them. After the incident at Pietsch's house, I listened to her husband's audio file."

"And? How damaging is it?"

She leaned in close and whispered what it was.

Pietsch would want to bury that. If it ever leaked, it could ruin her politically, and she had already announced her intent to run for senator. "Is her husband still one of your members?"

"He left after going through the unburdening session but before taking his vows. The councilwoman came and dragged him home, irate over how his joining would affect her politically. It was my understanding that he moved into the apartment above the garage and they are staying together for appearances."

"Thank you," he said with a sincere nod, understanding that she was putting herself at risk by talking. "You can be on your way."

"May the Light be upon you, Sheriff."

He gave Willa the signal, and she waved Miguel back to the vehicle.

After the Shining Light van pulled off, they climbed in the SUV.

"I felt bad for putting Fox through that after how hard I questioned him yesterday," she said. "I apologized for the inconvenience. Did Arlo give us anything?"

"Three names. All we need is for at least one of them to corroborate that McCoy blackmailed them for money, then we've got him."

"Do you want to hand this off to one of your deputies?" she asked.

"They've got their hands full following up on things related to the murder case." Besides, he wasn't sure if they would apply enough pressure to get the three to talk. They were wealthy and powerful and did not want their dirty laundry being aired. "Not much we can do until Livingston gets us contact information for the list of the Fallen. Our efforts this morning might be better served on this. If we have a chance to get McCoy, even a slim one, we have to take it." He put the SUV in Drive. "What do you say if I drop you off at your car and we can divide and conquer, each taking a name? We can join forces to tag team the last person later. I think it will take both of us."

"Who are we talking about?" she asked, curiosity gleaming in her eyes.

"Councilwoman Felicia Pietsch. Catching her off guard at her office might compel her to cooperate to keep any of her subordinates from overhearing."

"Interesting." Willa thought for a moment. "I think we should pay her a visit right now. Before she's coiffed and caffeinated. Without the armor of her makeup and a suit, it might be easier to get her to talk."

He trusted her judgment and was open to any ideas that would get them a cooperative witness. "Let's get an address for her."

WITH DANIEL STANDING beside her, Willa rang the doorbell of the Pietsch residence and braced herself for what was to come. She had to be convincing, more persuasive than ever before in her life. The pressure was immense to collar McCoy. She just hadn't realized she was on the clock with her career, her future, at stake because the mayor had lofty ambitions to be governor.

"We're closer now?" he said, the words sounding like a mix between a question and a statement, as he shifted his body so that she could see his full face.

For a heartbeat, she lost herself in his gaze. "To getting McCoy?" she asked, her voice a tad rough with her wondering if he was not discussing the case any longer, but in fact, their relationship. "Yes." She nodded, also answering the unspoken question in his eyes.

A crisp breeze sent a chill through her, making her shiver despite her zipped-up jacket.

Daniel gave her a half grin. "We can do this. Together."

"I hope you're right."

This was a gamble. Pietsch could throw them out of her house, slam the door in their faces and lawyer up.

Footsteps padded on the other side of the door before it swung open. A freckle-faced teenage girl stood facing them. Her light brown gaze fell to the star pinned to Daniel's shirt and swung to the badge on Willa's hip. "Mom! The cops are here!" She stood, holding the door until her mother hurried down the stairs.

Wearing fuzzy slippers and a robe that was open, revealing pink satin pajamas, a flustered Pietsch came to the door. "Go get dressed, honey," she said to her daughter, who scampered off. Yawning, she wiped the sleep from her eyes, her dark, messy hair looked as though she had just rolled out of bed. "What brings the sheriff and the chief of police to my door at such an early hour? I hope no one is hurt. Or dead."

"Ma'am," Daniel said. "May we come in?"

She appeared uncertain for a moment, then shook her head as if clearing a daze and stepped aside, opening the door wider. "Of course."

They both stepped into the foyer and removed their hats but kept their jackets on.

"Can I get you two some coffee? The machine is on a timer, and it hasn't perked yet, but I can switch it on and it'll be ready in a jiff."

They were going to pass on the coffee and not give her a reason to get up and leave the room once the conversation had started. "Ma'am, is there someplace where we can speak privately? Without your daughter overhearing?"

Her eyes grew wide with concern. "Yes, certainly. Follow me." She shuffled down the hall in her slippers, leading them to an office, and shut the door behind them. "What is this about?" she asked, fully awake now, and tied her robe closed.

Daniel gave her a look of pity. "Please, have a seat."

She stumbled to sit on a loveseat at the back of the room. Willa and Daniel grabbed chairs that faced the desk, turned them around, and sat.

"You're starting to worry me," Pietsch said. "Why are you here?"

"Did Marshall McCoy come to your home in June and blackmail you?" Willa asked. "Extort you for money?"

Bewilderment swept over her face. "I have no idea what you're talking about."

Willa narrowed her eyes, taking in every nuance of the woman's body language. "Are you saying he didn't come here?"

She crossed her legs at the ankles and folded her hands in her lap. "No, he paid me a visit. We had iced tea and a lovely chat."

"About what?" Daniel asked.

Uncrossing her legs, she licked her lips. "He asked me for a donation to help his organization."

"In exchange for keeping quiet about what your husband shared during his unburdening session," Willa said, a statement, not a question.

Her face paled and she swallowed, making an audible sound. "He did no such thing. Marshall is an upstanding citizen. A pillar of the community who has dedicated his life to helping the less fortunate."

"Ma'am, we're sensitive to your position." Daniel scooted to the edge of his chair and leaned in. "You're probably sweating bullets right now, fretting over how much we know, how it'll effect your reputation, your chances of winning a seat in the senate when it comes out that your husband defrauded investors of more than two million dollars and used some of that money to finance your campaign. The press will have a field day with it."

Pietsch pressed her lips tight and stiffened. Her eyes swam with guilt.

"You're not alone," Willa said, needing to hit her with an ice-cold dose of logic to make her see reason. "McCoy did this to others. This story is going to break. We're not here for your husband. Or for you. We want Marshall McCoy for extortion. Blackmail. Since there are others who are also guilty of something, the first one to speak might be able to cut a deal with the DA for immunity. If you're that person, then your husband would go to jail. Not you, if you got a deal."

Jennings loved to cut deals for immunity to get a witness to talk. This would give him the boon he needed for his political aspirations, but she seriously doubted that more than one person would get an offer.

"This will destroy any hope of a political future." Pietsch lowered her head and clutched her hands. "If you're here, then it means the DA doesn't have everything he needs. Not yet. Maybe not ever."

"Are you willing to take that chance?" Willa asked, drawing Pietsch's gaze back to her. "We know what your husband did. It's only a matter of time, days, possibly hours, before it's leaked. Once the press gets wind of this, you will be tried in the court of public opinion and the DA won't stop until there are convictions in a court of law." Not only for McCoy, but for whatever crimes the others had committed.

"If you can get immunity, you can get in front of this with the press," Daniel added. "Control the narrative rather than letting it control you."

"This doesn't have to be the end of your political career. People might see you as a victim if you were the one to turn your husband in and helped bring down McCoy." Anything was possible.

Daniel nodded. "He extorted a quarter of a million dollars."

"Someone is going to talk first. That person will fare the best. The others…" Willa shook her head. "This is survival of the fittest." She truly meant sleaziest. "Be smart. Be the first one to sit down with the DA. Tell us what happened."

Pietsch took a sobering breath and straightened, holding her head high. "Marshall did come to see me. *Me*, not Richard. He talked around what he was after. But honestly, I had no idea what Richard had told him while doped up on that drug they use. I had imagined an affair. Proof of multiple affairs. Then he asked Arlo to leave us alone. Things took a turn and got serious. Direct. He flat out told me that my husband had embezzled over two million dollars from his company and had used it to pay for the maintenance of his mistress, her condo, clothes, manicures, trips. To buy expensive toys, his watches, the suits. None of it would've played well in the press for me, but those things I could have survived. I mean if a president's wife can overcome her husband's affair to run for president herself one day, surely, I could rise above this. I refused to give him one cent."

Willa agreed. "How did McCoy take your refusal?"

"Not well. That's when I saw a different side to Marshall. He became vicious. Apparently, Richard had also funneled half of the illegal money into my campaign fund. Because he felt guilty about what a lousy husband he had been to me. But all he did was inadvertently tie me to his crime. I was so shocked and appalled to discover it that I didn't know what else to do besides write the check that Marshall wanted. Or he was going to leak the tape. I *am* the victim here."

Her story sounded good. Almost plausible. But Willa found it hard to swallow that she didn't know her husband had defrauded investors and given her one million dollars to help her win a senate seat. More believable was that they had worked out an arrangement that benefited them both.

Daniel shifted in his seat. "Did you ever tell your husband about McCoy's visit and the payment?"

"Of course. I was furious. The money came out of Paige's college fund."

The teen didn't deserve to suffer for her parent's mistakes, but millions took out student loans every year to pay for college. Willa had. "How did he respond?"

"He was horrified. Then he broke down in tears. After that I made him move his things to the apartment over the garage and end his affair."

"Richard didn't get angry about losing his

mistress?" Daniel asked. "Or about shelling out seventy-five thousand dollars to a man he had once trusted?"

"If he was angry, he didn't show it. Probably because I was mad enough to spit nails. He was apologetic. Dejected."

"Do you know where your husband was between ten and midnight on Sunday?" The autopsy report had narrowed the window for the time of death.

"Why?" Pietsch tensed.

"Do you know his whereabouts?" Willa pressed.

"He was here."

Daniel sighed. "How can you be sure if he was supposedly in the apartment above the garage?"

"Because he was in the living room camped out in front of the big-screen TV watching Sunday night football and drinking himself into oblivion. The last game started at eight p.m., I think. I was here, in the office, working until ten thirty, listening to him boo and clap. Sometime after eleven I told him to turn it down so I could sleep. Monday morning, I found him snoring on the sofa."

Willa glanced over to Daniel to see if he had any other questions. From the look he gave her, they were both satisfied. "Thank you, council-woman," Willa said.

"I'm going to call my attorney, get dressed and sit down with Allen Jennings this morning. I'll be damned if I let Richard's shenanigans torpedo my life."

Pressure ebbed from Willa's chest as she was one step closer to securing her job. "You're doing the right thing."

Chapter Eight

To Daniel's surprise, DA Jennings was not only willing to cut an immunity deal with Felicia Pietsch for turning in her husband for fraud and agreeing to testify against Marshall McCoy for blackmail, but the other two as well, provided they weren't guilty of murder or any crime involving a child.

Jennings was furious with McCoy for stealing his daughter. So much so that he wanted to get him on three counts of extortion and put him away for life more than he wanted to see the others behind bars.

By late afternoon, Roger Hines had also worked out a deal, but Elmer Clayborne had lawyered up and stuck to his story that his check for ninety-five thousand dollars—the largest of the three sums—had been a willing donation.

Neither were feasible suspects for the murders. Hines had stage four emphysema and couldn't get through a ten-minute conversation without requiring oxygen. While Clayborne was tough as nails, he was almost eighty-one and had a private nurse who tucked him into bed every night at 9:00 p.m.

They were certain they were looking for a big guy, athletic, under sixty, strong enough to carry an unconscious woman up to one mile, based on where bodies were found in relation to roads and the fact sedatives had been used. One smart enough to lure them into traps. A sharpshooter, if both killers were the same, with excellent accuracy.

"It'll be a relief once McCoy is behind bars," Willa said as they walked through the courthouse, heading toward the sheriff's department.

The hallway had a faint lemony smell that spoke of cleaning compounds. A scent he found oddly comforting. "A relief we'll have to wait for."

McCoy wasn't going to be arrested today. The DA had to get a few more pieces together first, but it would be soon. Maybe even tomorrow.

The question on Daniel's mind: Was Elmer Clayborne's sole concern getting through this unscathed, or would he give the cult leader a heads-up about the impending charges?

"Thanks to Arlo, and Mercy," Willa said, "that is one less thing to worry about. Now we can fully focus on finding our killer."

They reached the end of the hallway and turned left. Two doors down another corridor they came to the open set of double doors, with SHERIFF'S DEPARTMENT stenciled on the front.

Sweet home away from home.

Livingston was hard at work on the phone, talking and taking notes. After grabbing a bite to eat, Daniel wanted to start questioning the list of the Fallen.

Russo spun out of her chair and was on her feet, making a beeline toward them. "I've got good news and bad news."

Better a mix than purely the latter. "Bad news first."

"We widened the search radius for horse tracks at the crime scene for Gooding and Chavez. Both were a no-go, which leads me to believe the killer used a car and carried the victims to the site."

"Good news?"

"In widening the radius, we found two items. A necklace that must've fallen off the victim had DNA from Chavez on it. The other was a ring. Totally clean. No DNA and no prints on it. Based on where we found them, we can tell from which direction the killer approached the site, which leads to an auxiliary dirt road. No cameras."

Daniel swore under his breath. He was from Los Angeles, the most populous city in the United States with thirty-five thousand CCTV cameras. About nine for every thousand residents. There was a tiny fraction of that here, which didn't even cover every major intersection. When he didn't have a killer on the loose, he was grateful for the small-town feel, the slower pace, the tight community and the light traffic that didn't necessitate thousands of closed-circuit cameras.

But today, he had to tamp down his frustration.

"The two items are on your desk." Russo followed them into his office. "Father O'Neill at the church confirmed Fisher had been dropped off right before the start of an NA meeting. Some attendees helped get her inside. She was experiencing severe withdrawal symptoms at the time. They took her to the emergency room. The priest checked on her after she was discharged and got her to a shelter in Cheyenne. Sometime in late summer, he couldn't be sure exactly when, he spotted her back in town. Strung out and picking up johns at the truck parking lot across from the weigh station not far from the church. He encouraged her to come to the NA meetings, to get a hot meal that's offered once a day at their soup kitchen—they're open four days a week. He heard she was living in a tent near Cotton-wood Park."

"That's where we found her tent," Willa said.

"None of the employees at the bus station recall seeing any of the women," Russo said, "and nothing strange or out of the ordinary on the days they were dropped off there or in the vicinity. I'm heading over to try the truck park next. See if I can find any of Fisher's regulars. It's a two-minute walk from the bus stop. There might a connection between a trucker and all the victims."

Daniel picked up the sealed evidence bag that contained the necklace and looked it over. "It's worth a shot," he said as Willa grabbed the second bag. "Good work."

Livingston knocked on the door and waltzed in. "Got a minute?"

"Sure." Daniel glanced at Willa. Her forehead creased with unease as she stared at the ring in the bag, her skin turning pale.

"I've contacted all four individuals listed as the Fallen and departing the compound this year," Livingston said. "One guy, Roy Albertson is up in Montana. He left because his father passed away and one of the conditions of receiving his inheritance was that he had to manage the family ranch personally for five years and get married. Roy sounded happier than a pig in slop. After his dad disinherited him, he joined the Shining Light. His father's dying wish was to bring him back home."

"I guess it worked." Daniel put a hand on Willa's arm. "Everything okay?"

She nodded, but she looked the opposite. Not meeting his eyes, she set the bag down and faced Livingston.

"Alice Valdez and Louis Brooks chose to leave at the same time and are currently living together at her mother's house."

"What's their story?" Daniel cast a furtive look at Willa.

She folded her arms and appeared to be lost in thought.

"The two met and became a couple on the compound. But according to the cult's rules, unions are arranged based on the 'Light' speaking to Empyrean. Marshall McCoy had intended to separate them and match them to different partners. They weren't on board, so they left."

"Miguel Garcia mentioned that he was

matched with someone, as well. How are Alice and Louis doing? Happy like Roy Albertson?"

"Not quite." Livingston frowned. "Alice told me they fight all the time now and she regrets leaving the Shining Light. She wonders if Empyrean had been right about them not being a good match. Something to do with a karmic debt of their two souls and needing to heal spiritually with other partners. I didn't really understand what she was talking about. But she claims they were together with friends last weekend playing *Dungeons & Dragons* until the wee hours both Saturday and Sunday night."

"Maybe their relationship woes are a self-fulfilling prophecy. Someone told them that they were doomed to have trouble and now they read that into everything, trying to find it."

"I suppose." Livingston hiked up a shoulder. "Only one person on the list refused to talk to me." His gaze swung from Daniel to Willa. "Ezekiel Nelson. He's also the only person who joined the Shining Light four years ago *and* left this year," he said, and Willa remained stoic. "So I had a deputy bring him in. Nelson is sitting in the interrogation room, complaining that he has to fill in for a coworker tonight."

Awkward tension swelled in the room. "You made the right call." Daniel gave a little nod. "Can you give us a minute?"

"Sure thing." Livingston hurried out of the office, closing the door behind him.

"Talk to me," Daniel said and waited, but when she didn't respond, he closed the blinds to the window and turned back to her. "Why didn't you tell me that he joined four years ago?"

"I didn't think it mattered." Her voice was low.

"Of course it matters."

She looked up at him. "You think a seventeen-year-old kid was capable of being the Holiday Elk Horn Killer, responsible for viciously stabbing four women to death? Do you think my kid is capable of that?"

"What I think is that I should've heard it from you and not Livingston. You know as well as I it all comes down to the details. It's all important." But he felt like a fool for not reviewing the lists himself and simply trusting her.

"You're right." Turning, Willa gripped the edge of the desk and stared down at the evidence. "The ring…it's Zeke's."

Shock jolted through him. "What? Are you certain?"

"It was his father's class ring. Sterling silver with a dark black tone. Garnet center stone. Personalized side emblems and engravings. I gave it to him for his sixteenth birthday in the hopes it would encourage him to do better in school and graduate, to make his father proud. Yes, I'm sure." She shook her head, staring at it. "But I haven't seen him wearing it since he came home from the compound. There is a reasonable explanation for this. I know it. There has to be. My son is not a killer."

Daniel eased closer. "Do you know where he was the night of the murders?" he asked, wondering if he could even take her at her word.

"Sunday night I dropped him off at his grandmother's house, but the truth is, I don't know about the other evenings."

Her honesty was a relief. "Would you be willing to call the grandmother to see if he was there all night? On speaker?"

Willa's gaze lifted to his and she nodded without hesitation.

He put a hand on her shoulder and rubbed her arm. "Let's get to the bottom of this."

She picked up the receiver on his desk, dialed the number, and hit the speaker button. The line rang.

"Hello," the older woman answered.

"Irene, hi, it's me, Willa."

"Oh, I almost didn't pick up. I didn't recognize the number."

"I'm over at the sheriff's department working on a case. Hey, I had a quick question. After I dropped Zeke off on Sunday, did he stay there with you all night?"

The grandmother made a sound of exasperation. "Funny you should ask. Your son took my car after I told him *no* because I could smell the alcohol on his breath, and I was worried about him getting into an accident."

Willa grimaced. "What time did he come back?"

"Not until three in the morning. I am too old for this. He's going to give me a heart attack or a stroke from worrying about him. Later that morning I took him to pick up his own vehicle, which was parked outside a bar. I told him that if he wants to stay with me while the heat is out at his trailer and it's freezing over there, then he's going to have to start going to church with me. No ifs, ands or buts about it. And what does your son do? He goes running back to you because you'll tolerate his outrageous behavior. Spare the rod and spoil the child. You should have listened to me—"

"I've got to go." Willa squeezed her eyes shut. "Bye, Irene." She slammed the receiver down.

"I need to question Zeke. Now," Daniel said, heading toward the door.

"I'm coming with you."

"No, you're not. I'm bringing Livingston in with me."

She rocked back on her heels and stared at him in disbelief. "Why? That's my son we're talking about."

"Precisely. Someone in my office is feeding Jennings and/or the mayor information. There's no other way he found out about us questioning and releasing Miguel Garcia so fast. What do you think is going to happen the second he finds out that your son is a suspect? You can be in the observation room or stay in here until it's over. End of discussion."

Chapter Nine

Arms folded across her chest, Willa stood with her feet firmly planted, watching Daniel and Deputy Livingston interview her son through the one-way glass in the observation room that overlooked the interrogation room.

It was all surreal. Like a nightmare she couldn't wake up from. Zeke was troubled. Disrespectful. In pain. But he did not, could not murder one woman much less seven.

As the chief of police, related to the suspect, she didn't belong in the interrogation room. As a mother, willing to do anything for her child, there was no other place for her, but this was as close as she could get.

"Do you know Beverly Fisher?" Daniel asked as Livingston set a picture of the deceased down on the table.

Zeke reeled back in horror. "Oh, my God. No."

Willa licked her bone-dry lips, wishing she

had brought in a bottle of water. Her throat was parched, and a headache was starting to throb behind her eyes.

"Where were you the night of September 19th between ten p.m. and midnight?"

Her son shrugged. "I don't know. Can I see a calendar?"

Daniel looked at Livingston and nodded. The deputy pulled out his phone, tapped some buttons and showed Zeke the screen.

"I was off that day. I went to the Frontier Sports Bar," he said, and Livingston made a note. "I stayed until about one maybe."

"Can anyone verify that you were there?" Daniel asked.

"The bartender. A couple of waitresses. Patty for sure because she said I was a horrible tipper and needed to work on it."

Daniel nodded. "Do you know Leslie Gooding or Gemma Chavez?"

Zeke cringed at the next two photos the deputy put on the table. He looked away from them. "No. Is this why I'm here? You guys think I did this?"

Willa's chest ached at the resurgence of the pressure ballooning behind her sternum. If she could spare her son from looking at those photos—the horrendous images that would stick with him for the rest of his life—then she would. But showing suspects crime scene photos was a beneficial tactic that allowed the interviewers to gauge their initial response, which could be telling.

"We're not accusing you of anything," Daniel said. "We just need to get through these questions. What about this past Saturday? Where were you between ten and midnight?"

"I, uh, I was home. Alone."

Straightening, Daniel put his forearms on the table. "Home? In your trailer, where it's freezing cold because the heat has been shut off?"

Zeke looked up, past Daniel, to the one-way mirror. Her son's green eyes flared wide, anger giving color to his cheeks, and in that moment, he looked exactly like his father. "Did you tell your boyfriend that?" he said, and Livingston stared at Daniel. "Huh? What kind of mother betrays her son?"

Misery flooded her. This might be the breaking point in their relationship where he no longer wanted to have anything to do with her, even though she hadn't uttered a word about the lack of heat in his trailer. It didn't matter. Because he wouldn't believe her no matter what she told him.

"Hey." Daniel slapped the steel table. "Your mother has nothing to do with this interview."

"Interrogation! Call it what it really is."

Daniel took a breath. "Tell us about Sunday night. We know you weren't at Grandma's so don't bother lying."

Zeke scowled and lowered his head with a shake.

"Talk to me," Daniel urged. "Staying silent will not help you and it doesn't look good."

"Yeah, well, telling you where I was won't look good either."

"It's got to be better than looking like a murderer." Daniel leaned forward. "All I want is the truth."

"I was at Sheila Sanders's place."

What? That didn't make any sense. Willa prayed he wasn't lying. But if he wasn't, why would he be reluctant to give them an alibi?

"If I call Sheila Sanders, she's going to tell me that you were there with her?" Daniel asked.

Zeke shook his head. "I wasn't inside her place. I was at her place. Out front. In my car. Watching her through the window with Frankie Young."

Willa's skin crawled. Her son was a stalker? Hadn't she raised him better than that?

"Why were you there?" Daniel's tone was far gentler than hers would have been.

"We were on and off again in high school.

After the Shining Light, we hooked back up. But it was different. I don't know. Things had changed, but I told her I loved her and she said the words back. Then we had a fight."

Livingston stopped writing. "A physical altercation?"

"No. Mostly yelling. She shoved my chest once, but I didn't shove her back. Anyway, we decided to take a breather from each other. You know, give each other some space to clear our heads. I'm at the bar and Thomas told me she started seeing Frankie. But I didn't believe it because she made me swear that we wouldn't see other people during the break."

"Thomas got a last name?" Daniel asked.

"Mills," Zeke said, and Livingston made a note. "So I drove over there to see if it was true. Sure enough, they were snuggled up on the sofa watching horror movies. That's Sheila's classic MO to get a guy to make a move on her. She was encouraging him. Then I met up with Thomas for an early dinner before his shift on Sunday—"

"Where?" Livingston asked. "Time?"

"Pinky's Pizzeria. Around five. I was telling him all about it and in walks Frankie with his buddies. And I don't know what happened next. I like blacked out and when I came to Thomas was pulling me off him and Frankie's friends were helping him up. I warned him to stay away from Sheila. Then Wayward Bluffs police officers showed up and hauled me in for drunk and disorderly conduct. Later that night, I went back to see if he listened. The dude was there. Again. Watching another movie."

"Which ones did they watch?" Livingston asked, and Zeke rattled off two from some chainsaw or jigsaw series.

Zeke might be a stalker, but at least he had an alibi.

Daniel put the evidence bag with the ring on the table. "Do you know what that is?"

Her son picked up the bag and peered close. Surprise washed over his face. "Yeah, it's my dad's class ring. My mom gave it to me, but it was lost."

It was lost? Not he lost it?

Daniel scratched at the stubble on his jaw. "Lost when?"

With a shake of his head, Zeke shrugged. "I have no idea. When you decide to take your vows to the Shining Light and become a member of the community, you hand over all your possessions. I gave them my wallet, my clothes, my ring. It was liberating. But when I was forced to leave, they gave everything back. Except for the ring. They verified in the logbook that I had given it to them, but they couldn't tell me what happened to it. The ring was just gone."

The paper trail would corroborate what he said. It had to.

"Why were you kicked out?" Daniel asked.

"It's against the rules for one Starlight to strike another."

Fighting. Yet again.

How was it possible for her son to have so much anger when she had given him so much love? And why did he think he could solve his problems with his fists?

Even as a child he was quick-tempered and always got into scuffles on the playground.

"Who did you hit?" Livingston held his pen at the ready to jot down the name. "And why?"

"Fox from security," he said, and Willa groaned at the bad luck. "I was into this girl, Maria, and I thought she was into me, too. One day, Empyrean announced he was matching her and Fox together. I pulled her to the side and told her we shouldn't accept it. If we left, we could be together. She didn't want to. She thought Empyrean knew best. I didn't want to leave either. I loved it there, but every time I saw them together, smiling, holding hands, I just couldn't stop thinking, *Why is Fox getting what I should have?* I never should've hit him. I really hurt him, and he did nothing wrong. I apologized, but Empyrean said that my lack of acceptance would only fester and that I would be a problem for the community. So he made me leave. And every day since I've been back, I've hated Empyrean. Hated him for making me love that place and believe that new family would always be mine. Hated him for taking it all away without giving me a second chance. And I can't wait for him to get what he deserves someday and hurts the way he made me hurt."

Willa rubbed the back of her neck, wishing she could massage the ache from her chest. More than that, she longed for him to have love and happiness and inner peace. But he was never going to have any of it until she got him the help that he needed, and he started taking responsibility for his actions.

The door to the observation room swung open. Melanie Merritt, the deputy district attorney, walked in. "We have the warrant for Marshall McCoy's arrest."

"That was faster than expected. We didn't think your office would request one until tomorrow."

"We were working on charging him not only under the state law but also the federal blackmail statute. If we get the conviction on both counts, for Pietsch and Hines, he could receive up to twenty years in prison. Allen called in every favor to make this happen as soon as possible. He doesn't want the great Empyrean to spend one more night in his plush bed. He wants to dethrone him tonight."

Arresting McCoy would ruffle plenty of feathers on the compound. No one would want to cooperate with her, letting her simply look at their inventory register for the belongings of new recruits after they slapped handcuffs on their Empyrean.

It wasn't enough that Zeke had an alibi. She needed to prove that the ring wasn't in his possession at the time of the murders. The only way to do that without waiting for a warrant of her own was to go ahead of Daniel to the compound.

"You should know that us getting McCoy is like having a weight off the shoulders of my office," Melanie said. "We can all breathe again. Thanks to you and Sheriff Clark."

"We didn't do it alone. Mercy McCoy and Arlo Starlight helped."

"Arlo? I'd assumed she'd gone dark forever."

"She was afraid of hurting everyone on the commune if they lost the tax-exempt status. The sheriff got her to see that there's more than one way to skin a cat. Excuse me, I have to take care of something. Would you let the sher-iff know that I'll meet him at the compound?"

"No problem."

Willa hurried out the door and down the hall.

THE CROWD OF protesters at the front gate of the compound had tripled in size as the mayor had predicted. The chants through the bull-horns boomed around her as she pulled up to the guardhouse.

After rolling down her window, she and the guard yelled back and forth, keeping it short, and she was waved through the gate.

Her cell buzzed. It was Daniel.

She put the call through the Bluetooth. "This is Nelson."

"Spare me the formality," he snapped, sounding annoyed. "What are you doing?"

"Getting the evidence my son needs to clear his name."

"We can get a warrant for it tomorrow."

Not good enough. She was going to ensure that her son didn't have to spend the night in jail without worrying about backlash from the mayor or the DA on how they had released yet another suspect. "Why wait when I can get it tonight? You should be praising my efficiency. By the time you arrive, I'll have it."

"We're supposed to be a team. Doing this together."

"I've got to go." She disconnected.

Despite the intrusion to their dinner, Sophia was waiting at the bottom of the stone steps in front of Light House along with Huck.

"What can I do for you, Chief Nelson?" she asked as Willa vacated the SUV, raising her voice to speak over the chants of the protesters.

"When my son, Ezekiel, left this August, he said that he was supposed to be given back all his possessions, but a ring he had was missing. Can we see if any notes were made in the inventory list?"

Sophia looked to Huck, but they nodded in unison. "I see no reason why we can't accommodate that request. Right this way." Sophia started walking and Huck ascended the steps, going into Light House. She keyed the radio. "Shawn, could you meet me at the shed with the key?"

"I'm coming now," the head of security said.

"At what point, is someone required to hand over their belongings?" Willa asked.

"Nothing is required here. Everything is a choice. We encourage everyone to go through the process of exuviation—the casting off their former selves in preparation to become something and someone new—as soon as they feel ready to do so. Some shed their belongings as soon as they arrive, even if they don't become members. But every recruit who has decided to fully embrace the Light and take their vows has already done this well in advance."

Willa dug deep not to roll her eyes. "Do you ever sell any of the member's possessions?"

"Definitely not. If for some reason a member must leave us, then we wish to restore them as they came to us."

"Does that include money?"

A coy smile. "We don't give back donations."

They went around to the back side of the garage and stopped at a building that was roughly half the size of the ten-bay garage. Although the overall shape resembled that of a shed, the name was misleading.

Shawn ran over, meeting them at the door. He input the code on the keypad and with a beep, the red locked light flashed green.

"Who has access to the shed?" Willa asked.

"Most members of the security team, ma'am. It gives us the flexibility to open it without delay whenever a member departs." He opened the door for them, and they stepped inside.

Sophia hit the light switch, illuminating rows and shelves filled with boxes of tagged items.

"How does the process work when a member leaves?"

Sophia turned to a shelf with books lined up in chronological order by the year printed on the spine and grabbed one. "We find out what year they arrived," she said, opening it and flipping through the pages, "find their name." She stopped on Ezekiel's. "Everything is listed and the member initials it. We tag everything and store it. When they are ready to go, we use the serial number on the tag to locate the items, turn them over, and the member departs."

The initials *EN* were beside each meager personal thing he'd described in detail.

"Here's the note," Sophia said, pointing it out. "His ring couldn't be located. Someone from security searched for twenty minutes. It's odd and quite rare for something to go missing."

"I'll need a copy of that page in the ledger," Willa said, and Sophia looked prepared to protest. "But if that's going to be a problem, I'll simply be back tomorrow with a warrant."

"Shawn." Sophia handed him the book. "Please make a copy for Chief Nelson."

With a curt nod, he took the ledger and hustled off.

"It'll only be a moment."

Willa looked around. It would be easy

enough for someone who was waiting to receive their belongings to slip their hand in a box and swipe an item from the shelf, especially something as small as a ring, if the security guard's back were turned for only a few seconds.

"I'm sorry I intruded on your dinner," Willa said.

"You didn't. We're always finished by seventy thirty."

"How is it coming with that list of individuals who have been here awhile without taking vows?"

"It's coming. The sheriff did give us forty-eight hours."

That he did. "Are you truly happy here?"

Sophia flashed a genuine smile that reached her eyes. "It's the closest to paradise on earth. On our compound, there's no violence, no rape, no murder. Everyone is treated with dignity and respect. We seek to enlighten and as we improve ourselves, make the world a better place."

Sounded good in theory. For those who had lived and thrived on the compound for decades that might have been true, but Willa was struggling with how broken her son had been after being cast out of this paradise. The animosity he had toward Marshall McCoy concerned her, but if her son felt that way, there must have been others. It made her wonder, what if the killer wasn't one of the Fallen, or a guy on the compound, but someone else? They were missing something.

Shawn returned with the copy and locked up while Sophia walked her back to her vehicle. By the time they reached her SUV, the genuine smile on the young woman's face dissolved as two sheriff's vehicles came up the drive with flashing lights that indicated this would be a different kind of visit.

The front door of Light House flew open, and Huck hurried down the steps. Marshall McCoy, his last day clad in an all-white suit, appeared in the doorway and moseyed down as though they couldn't possibly be there for him. In his mind, he must have thought himself untouchable.

Daniel slid her an irritated glance and she held up the copy of the document. Shaking his head at her, he handed Huck the warrant and strode past him up to the mighty Empyrean. "Marshall McCoy, you're under arrest for blackmail," Daniel said, handcuffing him as he read him his Miranda rights.

Pale as death, obviously in shock, McCoy looked to Huck to get him out of this.

All the lawyer said was, "I'll meet you at the station."

There would be no wiggling out of this one. Jennings had made certain before getting the warrant.

Russo and Livingston took McCoy by the arms and got him into the back of the SUV. Their presence was starting to draw a crowd of onlookers.

Sophia stood, gaping and trembling in disbelief as Starlights gathered around her, watching as their Empyrean was hauled off in cuffs.

Daniel strode up to her, his expression stern, but she wasn't going to apologize.

"Did you release Zeke?"

"Yeah, I did. We'll verify everything he told us, but he's not going anywhere. In fact, he was on his way to work to relieve a coworker who needed to leave early. Livingston called the gas station and confirmed it."

"Here you go." She gave him the copy. "Jennings is happy with us for now, but neither of us needs the mayor making a stink out of this."

He sighed. "I don't want to argue with you."

"Then don't." She grinned at him, and his mouth lifted in a slight, reluctant smile. "We've both been up since five this morning. I'm famished and can hear your stomach growling. How about we have another working dinner, but with less work." Far less since Zeke wouldn't intrude tonight. "I've got a theory I want to run by you."

"I'm in. But I need to be at the station when we process McCoy and see if he'll make a statement."

"He won't. Huck won't let him say a word."

"My thoughts exactly."

"Want to do dinner at your place or mine?"

"Yours. You've got the tasty leftovers. I'll even build a fire," he said, and she shivered, not from the cold, but pure anticipation. "Provided McCoy stays silent, I won't be far behind you."

"I need to swing by Zeke's job and check in on him. See how he's doing."

"Take care of your kid. That's got to come first."

He really was the best. Almost too good to be true. *Almost.* "See you soon."

Chapter Ten

After Marshall McCoy had been booked and shown into the interrogation room, Daniel sat in front of him and his lawyer, Huck.

"I exercise my right to remain silent," McCoy replied to the fifth question.

"Is it true that you used the money you received from Pietsch, Hines and Clayborne to pay off the back taxes on the compound?"

"I exercise my right to remain silent," he repeated, staring down at the table, looking bored.

This was a golden opportunity, having McCoy down at the station. Daniel decided not to waste it. "Did you ask or authorize someone on the compound to kill Beverly Fisher, Leslie Gooding and Gemma Chavez?"

McCoy's gaze flicked up to his. "No."

Daniel had just been fishing to see if the man would bite. "Did the murders of those women keep your flock from running after Mercy rejected you and your movement?"

Huck turned to him with worry stamped on his face, a muscle working in his jaw.

"No," McCoy said plainly, and the lawyer whispered to him, whatever he was saying was accompanied by enthusiastic hand gestures.

"Do you know who killed Fisher, Gooding and Chavez?"

Lowering his gaze, McCoy returned to playing the silence game.

"Do you have suspicions as to who it could be?" Daniel asked.

They were back to more of the same, and this was why Daniel hated having lawyers present during interviews. Invariably, it made his job harder.

Daniel was willing to bet that he could've gotten more out of McCoy. The killer was tied to the Shining Light somehow, which meant Marshall either knew who he was or could help lead them to him. "The court might show you some leniency if you identified the serial killer. More innocent lives could be lost. Lives you can save by giving me a name." Daniel stared at him, waiting, hoping. "You make yourself out to be a savior but you're nothing more than a hypocrite." He shoved to his feet. "You'll spend the night here in a holding cell. Tomorrow you will be remanded to the county jail until your bail hearing."

"I'd like my one phone call," Marshall said.

"Your lawyer is already here."

"Clearly."

Huck could pass along any message he wanted back on the compound. "Who do you want to call?"

"My daughter."

Huck stared at him with as much surprise as Daniel felt. "I'll see that you get your phone call."

"And her number. I'll need that as well," McCoy said.

With a curt nod, Daniel left the room and headed to his office. For a minute, he'd gotten the man talking. How? Was it because Daniel had been asking the right questions? Or the wrong ones?

"The mayor is on line one for you," Livingston said.

Groaning, Daniel scrubbed a hand over his face. "Did anybody get me what I needed?" he asked to the other deputies in the bullpen.

Mitch Cody, the prior army helicopter pilot Daniel had persuaded to join the department, hopped up, rushed over and handed him a piece of paper. "Thomas Mills confirmed Zeke's statement. Sheila Sanders did watch the movies named with Frankie Young. The waitress Patty Weber couldn't remember if he was there on the 19th, but she said he never pays in cash, always credit card, making it easy for us to verify, and he is a horrible tipper."

Armed with that and the documentation Willa had procured, showing that the ring in question had been lost or stolen on the compound and not returned to the kid, should be enough ammunition.

"YOU WERE THERE behind the one-way mirror, watching me being grilled weren't you, Mom?"

Denying it wouldn't help either of them. She didn't want a relationship built on lies. "I was."

Zeke glared at her from behind the counter at the gas station in Wayward Bluffs. "And you did nothing to help me. In fact, you violated my trust and told them my heat was shut off."

"I said nothing about your trailer or the status of your bills." Taking a breath, measuring her words, she put her hands on her hips. She was grateful to be free of the weight of her duty belt she'd left in her vehicle. "Listen to me. I know you're not a murderer. I believe in you. Always have and always will. You mean the world to me. I also have faith in the system and this is how it works. Questioning is a part of it."

"You could've advised me to keep my mouth shut and gotten me a lawyer."

He was right. She could have. "Then you would still be under suspicion, and I would have been forced to recuse myself from this case. You answered the sheriff's questions and—"

"Don't you mean your boyfriend?"

Ignoring that, she continued. "And I got the proof from the compound that your ring was never returned to you. Once they verify everything else you've told them, you'll be officially cleared. Which is a much faster, cheaper and more efficient way than hiring an overpriced lawyer." That took some of the steam out of him. "The mayor is scrutinizing this case closely. Schroeder will not like it that you were released. I know you don't care if I lose my job over it, but there's a lot at stake." She pulled her wallet from her pocket, fished out three twenty-dollar bills and slapped them down on the counter. "Pay your gas bill, apologize to your grandmother for taking her car without permission and don't you ever drink and drive again. Not only can you end up wrapped around a tree, but you could also kill someone else. You're smarter than that. Start acting like it." She turned to leave, then hesitated. "What do you have to say for yourself?"

"Thanks. Not just for this," he said, picking up the cash. "And I do care if you lose your job. I just don't want what happened to Dad to happen to you."

He still carried the grief of losing Zach, but she didn't want him to fear that the same would happen to her.

"I love you," she said, turning for the door, not expecting him to say anything in return.

"Ditto," he grumbled behind her.

Smiling, she climbed into her SUV and headed home. Normally after a tough day and working a case she needed to crack, she'd go to the gym. Get in thirty minutes of vigorous cardio and weightlifting to keep her muscles toned and her body strong. Once she got into a zone, her mind would empty and any issues she had resolving a case would start to unravel.

Tonight, she wanted company—Daniel's— and conversation instead cardio, though she was open to getting sweaty with him. It was nice to have someone in her corner, who she could rely on. A hot cowboy and a cop all rolled into one.

Not much farther now. This last road would take her home. She wondered if she'd have time to shower before Daniel arrived.

Willa took the corner way too fast, and her SUV's tires slid a bit, but she corrected. She'd been on this hilly road hundreds of times in all sorts of weather, even blizzards, but she was exhausted and starving, driving a tad too aggressively. She took another bend in the road and began to slide, lucky to finagle her way out of it before the SUV hit the shoulder and careened over the side into the gorge that was Devil's Canyon.

She shifted down, slowing. The tires slid again as though the road was slick with black ice close to the top of the hill. *Not that cold yet.* Only a little farther to go and she'd be headed down the hill, toward home. She'd be there in minutes.

Hopefully, Zeke was all right.

Once more the vehicle slipped, the wheels losing their grip. It had been a while since she had replaced them. Low tread could reduce tire traction. Maybe that was the prob—

Crack!

The canyon echoed the blast of a high-powered rifle shot—the sound unmistakable to her.

Gut instinct made Willa duck. Her SUV shuddered. Someone was shooting at her vehicle.

Keeping one hand on the steering wheel, she fumbled for her firearm that was in the passenger seat on her duty belt. Then it occurred to her what was actually happening.

Those weren't just shots at her.

It's the Holiday Elk Horn Killer. This is how he first isolates his victims. Shooting out their tires.

Oh, God!

Fear speared her heart.

She had to make it down the hill, beyond the canyon. Almost, almost. She was almost there, but the tires hit another slick patch.

It wasn't cold enough for ice. Was it oil?

The SUV spun, tires skidding. Her seat belt gripped tight, digging across her chest, and there wasn't anything she could do behind the wheel.

Faster and faster her vehicle whirled. She had to do something before it was too late. Frantically, she snatched her cell from the magnetic mount on the dash and dialed Daniel, but the phone slipped from her hand as the SUV slammed into the guardrail.

Metal shrieked and groaned, giving way, and the SUV slid over the edge. All she could do was hang on and pray she didn't die. The drop into the forest—*thank God not the canyon*—was only a few feet, but her vehicle tipped, landing on its side and rolled.

With the crunch of steel and shattering glass, she pitched forward at the same time the airbag deployed. It slammed her back against the seat, pressing hard against her face and chest. Pain ripped up her neck and shoulder. The scream of twisting metal filled her ears. Sharp rocks and debris tore through the broken windows. The front panels crumpled. A tire popped during the roll down the slope.

She couldn't focus on the warm blood that oozed from the side of her head. The vehicle flipped over, landing upside down. The roof crunched on impact, jarring Willa to her bones.

Fire whipped through her shoulder. The airbag squeezed her tight, the grit from its deployment making her eyes burn.

Agony fogged her brain. Her lungs were tight, so tight it was though the air was being squeezed from her lungs. Cool night air whipped through the car. She could barely think, barely breathe, but she fought to stay conscious.

The killer was out there, the hunter. Watching. Making his way to her. To stalk his prey.

Awareness slid over her. She still held her sidearm. That was something.

If he dared approach her while she was trapped in the SUV, she'd shoot to kill. No questions asked.

This was bad. Dire.

Get out. Now! Get out and run!

She pressed on the release button of her seat belt and tried to push the airbag from her face. Neither would budge. Pain rippled up her shoulder and she let out a wounded yelp. Something was wrong with the airbag—a defect in the construction or a mechanical error.

Despair welled inside her.

Come on. Think. You're running out of time.

He was out there. Somewhere in the darkness. Moving closer. She sensed his presence like an ominous shadow slithering overhead. His intention was clear and deadly.

All she could think about were the first victims on Elk Horn. Images of them flashed through her mind. Stripped and tied, their wrists bound so tightly to tree trunks that their skin was bruised and broken. Their chests stabbed. Throats slashed. Bitten. Dead. Skin gray. Brunette hair fanned out like a crown.

Nausea punched through her stomach as she realized she fit the profile of the first victims. Aged twenty to forty. Slim. White. Dark hair. Single. Driving alone when he struck.

No, no, no! She couldn't let that happen to her. *Move! Get the hell out!*

Groaning against the pain, she shoved her fingers down and pushed hard on the seat belt release button. Nothing.

She jabbed down on it harder, again and again. But it was no use. It was jammed.

Ice-cold panic flooded her veins. At any moment that sick murderer would pop up, a nightmare made flesh and blood, and stuck in this position, trapped by the air bag, she was a sitting duck. It would be the end of her.

She listened for approaching footsteps, snapped twigs, any noise that would give him away. But he was hunting a cop. Not just any officer but the chief of police. He had the audacity and the smarts to set the perfect trap. He'd expect her to be armed and she expected him to be prepared.

Teeth chattering from the pain and the fear, she struggled to wrangle her thoughts.

Don't give up! Keep fighting!

If she could move the air bag enough to breathe or reach her phone or…

The knife in her pocket.

Grimacing through the throbbing ache, she struggled to slip her hand into her pocket and reach her Buck Budgie. Swallowing back her panic, she shoved her fingers deeper. The tips grazed steel. *Almost. Come on.* Frantically— adrenaline driving her to hurry—she gritted her teeth and eased her hand farther.

Any second she expected him to appear.

Her heart pounded furiously, beating hard as

a drum. Desperation and anger swept through her as she clenched the knife. *Yes! Thank God.*

Sharp and sturdy, the blade would set her free. She pulled the knife to her chest slowly, so it didn't fall through her fingers. Hands shaking, she slipped open the blade with her left hand clenched around her gun. Furiously, she stabbed the air bag.

After a *pop*, it hissed and slowly deflated. The strong chemical smell it left behind tainted the air, making her cough. She shoved the collapsed bag out of the way and started on the seat belt. If not for her injured shoulder, she would have made quick work of slicing through it. As it was, the sawing motion took effort, adding pressure to her rotator cuff, and irritating her bruised flesh.

Sawing through the seat belt, she sensed rather than saw she wasn't alone. She turned her head to look around and grimaced. Hurting all over, she was one hell of a mess. But alive.

She had to get out if she intended to stay that way.

Listening again, she didn't hear anything besides the howling wind and her wild heartbeat. In the darkness, she only saw trees, the ground, and shadows playing tricks on her mind.

But she knew he was out there. Watching and waiting.

She aimed the gun out the window, hoping to get a glimpse of him. *Show yourself.*

Seconds ticked by in her head matching the rhythm of her pounding heart.

Nothing.

She turned back to the seat belt. Her only thought now was to hurry and get out. Moving faster—the pain making her vision blur—she continued sawing until the belt broke free and she dropped to the roof.

Agony exploded through her shoulder, her spine, her neck. Tears burned behind her eyes. Her shoulder was dislocated. The gut-wrenching sensation was familiar. She had an old injury that flared up if her shoulder was hit with enough force at the wrong angle. Hands trembling badly, she managed to close the knife and stuff it in her pocket. Shifting her Glock to her right hand, she braced herself to crawl over the broken glass and out of the vehicle. But once she did, she'd be exposed with no more cover.

He might be waiting for her to make that very move.

A sharp prick stung the back of her leg.

What in the hell?

Had she cut herself? She touched her hamstring and felt something small and metallic lodged in her muscle.

She yanked it out and stared down at a dart

with a tiny needle. Her heart turned to a block of ice.

Oh, no. He shot her with something worse than a bullet. There was no telling what kind of drug was inside the tiny silver cartridge. If she stayed there, giving it time to work through her system, it was all over.

Panic-stricken, she searched for her phone to call for help. But she didn't see it anywhere. Had it been thrown from the car? She swore under her breath. Where was her duty belt?

She shoved a branch that was in the car aside and found it. Grabbing her radio, she keyed the transmit button. "This is Chief Nelson."

"Go ahead, Chief," the duty officer replied.

"I'm in imminent danger. I rolled over off Route 4 less than two miles from my home," she said, and it struck her like a bolt of lightning that this sick monster knew where she lived. How long had he been following her? Stalking her? Planning this? Since she was first in the news making a statement about Fisher? But why now? Were they close to finding him? "I believe the Holiday Elk Horn Killer is after me. He blew out my tires, causing my vehicle to go off the road, and shot me with some kind of tranquilizer dart." Medetomidine. That's what he used. "Contact Sheriff Daniel Clark. He may be the closest to me to respond immediately. Send backup. Proceed with caution. He slicked the road with something and he is armed and dangerous."

A crack shot for sure, to disable her car and send it careening off the road. An ace marksman. A hunter.

"Yes, ma'am," the duty officer said and switched over to a different line for a moment and then returned. "Can you see him, Chief?"

"No. But he's out there." Closing in. Hunting her. Time was running out. She had no idea how long it would take before she was incapacitated. If she didn't move now, she was going to die here. "I'm moving from the wreckage of my vehicle." He'd expect her to continue downhill, where the ground plateaued. It made the most sense. So she was not going to do what he expected. "I'm injured, but I'm going to try heading back uphill toward the road," she said.

Willa pictured him waiting for her in the darkness. Patiently. Quietly. Finger on the trigger, ready to put a bullet in her chest. But then he wouldn't have bothered to drug her.

She forced herself to crawl out of the car through the busted window. Shards of glass bit into her left palm that she used to pull herself forward.

Blinking hard through the pain, she stood and brought up her pistol. She turned three-sixty, scanning the woods for him. Numbness seeped through her. Holding the weapon up was getting harder. Already her fingers and limbs were having trouble responding as a tingle spread through her.

The sedative was working fast. Too fast.

A howl broke the quiet. It sounded like a wolf, but it had been made by a man. Of that she was certain.

That predator was coming for her.

But she wasn't going to make it easy. Holding tight to her gun, heart drumming, Willa ran.

Chapter Eleven

Punching the accelerator, his SUV fishtailing, Daniel straightened out the wheels with some effort. He took the winding road, which had been made even more treacherous with a slippery substance, as hard and fast as he dared. The point was to find her, not to get into a wreck himself. He kept hoping for a glimpse of Willa's car, any sign of her or an accident.

He glanced at the GPS. Three miles from her house. In the middle of nowhere. Why did she live in such a remote, isolated area in Wayward Bluffs?

Space, privacy and few neighbors but they're all nice, she'd told him.

He cursed every single one of her reasons now, even though he couldn't throw a rock from his place and hit any of his neighbors' houses.

Where are you, Willa?

His SUV slid, sending his pulse skyrocketing, and he tapped the breaks, careful not to go into a spin. He'd finally reached the slickness she had mentioned. As much as he ached to slam on the gas and get to her as soon as possible, he had to slow it down. Just enough to avoid getting into a wreck himself.

Two and half miles from where he expected to spot her or her vehicle.

There had been no mention of any slick substance found on the road near the victims' cars in the cold case files. But the killer wouldn't have needed it with civilians. Taking on Willa, on the other hand, a trained professional, the guy was probably stacking the deck in his favor. Handicapping her as much as possible to ensure he got his prey.

Daniel slapped the steering wheel. If they'd gone together, had left at the same time, then this wouldn't be happening.

But there would have been another moment, sooner or later, when she would be vulnerable and unsuspecting and alone. Then this predator still would have pounced. Tonight—*thank God*—Daniel had planned to come out here and was already on the way, and Zeke was out of harm's way, safe at work. If nothing else, Daniel estimated that he wasn't too far behind Willa based on the time the call came through about her accident.

Rounding another bend, his headlights swept over a busted portion of the guardrail—gnarled steel split wide.

That's where she must have gone off the road and over the side. His gut clenched. How far was the drop? Noting the mile marker, he slowed to a stop and threw the vehicle into Park.

Hopping out and treading carefully around the vehicle, he got on the radio. "This is Sheriff Clark. I've found where Chief Nelson was forced off the road. Route 4, mile marker 7." He popped the trunk and grabbed his emergency roadside kit.

"Copy, Sheriff. Notifying inbound units, the ambulance and your helicopter pilot."

The wind shrieked in the surrounding canyons, sounding too much like a wounded animal. His mind was playing tricks on him. He was just keyed up and needed to focus on the only thing that mattered right now. Finding Willa.

He unzipped the bag and grabbed a road flare. After locating the rough striking surface on the cap on one end of it, he tore off the plastic lid. He held the flare away from his face and lit it much the same way he would strike a match.

The flare sprayed ignited, molten material

that would burn for an hour. He tossed it a hundred feet behind his SUV, where approaching vehicles would easily spot it. He hurried forward, past the SUV, toward the mangled opening in the guardrail.

His thoughts took a dark turn as he considered his father, James Clark, and his final minutes. On a road not too different from this one. Also, here in Wyoming. Near Laramie in the Snowy Range Mountains. A brutal storm. Poor visibility. A tragic accident where his car had gone over the side of an embankment. Died on impact before Grace had even been born.

But that was twenty-six years ago. The past would not repeat itself. There was no storm, no mischance at work here.

This was the cunning machination of a vicious serial killer. Willa was alive, fighting for every breath, and she needed him.

Clutching his kit, he rushed to the opening and peered over the side. Trees and darkness spread as far as the eye could see. The bloated moon was bright and the sky clear, but the woods were so dense the moonlight didn't hit the forest floor.

Where the hell is she? He didn't even see her damaged vehicle. Not because the drop had been too far, but because it had rolled. The savage bulldozed path the wreckage had cut made him wonder how bad the accident was and how serious her injuries might be.

Worry gnawed at his insides, reminding him that every time he found a sliver of happiness it had slipped right through his fingers, like grains of sand he couldn't hold on to.

Not this time. Not today.

After two long, long years, fate had brought Willa back into his life, and she was the best thing to have happened to him since he'd moved out here at the age of eighteen and learned what it meant to be a cowboy. From the second she'd flashed her badge in Crazy Eddie's he'd been drawn to her like a dying man in the desert to a lush oasis.

"Hell," Daniel grunted. He had it bad. It was a wonder how she'd managed to have gotten under his skin so quickly. *You let her, you fool. Now look at you.* She'd slipped in a while ago when their no-promises, no-strings-attached fling had evolved into a full-blown affair. Only he hadn't realized it until she had cut him off completely before they'd started to border on a relationship.

And that's what he wanted with her. A relationship. Cooking together. Cuddled up in front of the fire. Supporting one another. Building each other up. He wanted to be a haven for her.

But there was a killer on the loose who had put her in his sights.

Dread caused stomach acid to bubble up his throat. Scanning the terrain below, he searched for any sign of her. Still, nothing. Desperation sent him shuffling down the side of the hill without any gear to prevent him from falling if he took a nasty stumble.

Another blast of wind shrieked through the canyon. Listening closely, it sounded like a wolf howling. Urgency pounded through him as he scurried along the rocky terrain. His mind was racing, his heart throbbing with a mix of fear and fury.

DARKNESS DANCED AROUND the edge of her vision. She blinked, fighting it, and an image of Daniel floated in front of her. Relationships ended badly for her. Once nearly tragically. Perhaps this was the universe's way of telling her that Daniel would be good to her and good for her—body, mind and soul—but to balance the scale, this was how she would meet her end. At the hands of a sadistic madman.

Daniel's face vanished, but he was coming for her. Help was on the way. She simply had to hang on, keep moving, keep fighting. She scrambled up the slope, her body slow, her footing unsteady. Her shoulder was in agony, but she clung to the pain, grateful it was the only thing preventing her from succumbing completely to the drug coursing through her veins. But not for much longer. The adrenaline, the stark fear, wasn't enough anymore. It was getting harder and harder to clamber up the hill. To hold…on to…her gun. She shook her head, desperate to clear the fogginess.

She stumbled and swayed before she dropped to her knees. Unable to make herself stand back up, her brain refusing her commands, she tipped backward, hitting the ground.

Blinking hard, she was starting to fade. Numbness crept through her limbs, her mind clouding.

Her head lolled to the side, as she tried to look for the devil. Her fingers loosening around the gun until her grip was no more and her firearm slipped free.

The sky began to spin—the world, the moon dimming.

"Chief Nelson," he said, turning her heart to stone. His tone was congenial and warm like he knew her.

He was close. Only a few feet away.

"No," she said, her voice shallow, her tongue thick, her throat dry.

This was her son's greatest fear, losing her

to the darkness of the job. She couldn't die like this. For Zeke's sake. She had to survive to repair the dysfunction between them, to give him a chance at the future he deserved. She had to truly start living herself, letting in love, giving herself permission to be happy. Not only preach the way, but show him, leading by example.

She struggled to find her weapon. But failed.

It was there. On the ground beside her. Somewhere…somewhere. She was starting to slip beneath the surface of consciousness.

"Looks like you're having car trouble. Do you need help?" he asked, taunting her.

This was what he had probably said to his victims, getting them to lower their guard, letting him get close. But he was just toying with her. For sport.

And then he came into view, his features covered by a ski mask, night vision goggles shielding his eyes. A figure in black painter's coveralls.

"Want me to give you a hand?" he asked, extending his toward her. Metal glinted in his other hand. A large, hunting knife.

Chilling, bone-deep terror sliced through her.

Mustering the last of her waning strength, she growled at him as she extended her fingers, feeling around for her pistol. "Drop dead."

"Not before you," he said in a singsongy

voice that gave her chills. "But first, we're going to have some fun. At least, I am."

"Go to hell." Battling the sluggishness overtaking her more and more every second, she groped for her Glock. This time her fingers hit cold steel. She heaved it up into the air. If only she could aim. She fired.

Pop, pop, pop.

But all the shots had missed, flinging up dirt and breaking off bits of bark from a nearby tree. No, no, no.

"Aww, that's too bad, Chief. Nice try, though. I'll give you an A for effort."

"Cheater." The word lacked the force she had longed to hurl at him.

The only way he could win against her was by slicking the road, shooting out her tires, drugging her from a distance.

Coward.

She raised the gun to squeeze off another round, but her fingers didn't respond. Unconsciousness clawed at her, threatening to suck her under. "Can't win…a fair…fight."

He kicked her sidearm from her hand and stepped on her forearm, dragging a scream from her. As he eased off the pressure, the darkness swooped in, determined to swallow her, and the fear evaporated, leaving only sharp-edged doggedness to end this man's life, if by some miracle, she ever got the chance.

A SERIES OF gunshots echoed through the canyon. Slowing his descent, Daniel pinpointed the direction of origin.

There. Her car. Crushed metal caught the light of the moon. He swept his gaze slowly, steadily up the hillside from there.

Willa! Oh, God. Was someone beside her?

His heart squeezed as he realized that the killer was right on top of her. Willa's agonizing scream carried on the wind, echoing in the woods, ripping through him. Every muscle in his body tensed as a rush of adrenaline flooded through his veins. His need to reach her before it was too late was single-focused and overwhelming. Racing like a madman down sloped terrain, he scrambled faster to get to her, his chest tight, feeling like his lungs might burst.

Daniel wended through the thicket of drooping evergreens, heading down the razed path her car had made. Pulse pounding, muscles burning, he hurried, needing to do something. *God.* If he didn't reach her in time…

Frantic, his breath punching from his mouth, Daniel slid several feet, narrowly catching hold of a tree trunk to stop his rapid-fire descent. He was close enough now that he could more clearly make out the twisted metal of her wrecked car and details of her assailant. Tall. Medium build. Cloaked in black. And wearing night vision googles.

Cold fear tightened in his gut. He dug into the emergency kit and pulled out another flare. Quickly, he used the striking surface on the cap to light it and threw it. The flare, spitting molten sparks, landed near Willa and in her attacker's eye line because the monster reeled back like the bogeyman from the light.

Daniel drew his sidearm. At the same time, the helicopter swooped in overhead, piloted by his deputy Mitch Cody. The aircraft's bright spotlight shone on the killer. Daniel took aim and fired. Once. Twice. Three times. The third shot jerked him forward, like he'd been hit or grazed on the left arm. Then the predator disappeared in the forest, evading the helicopter's searchlight in the trees.

Daniel rushed the rest of the way down, panting and filled with dread, his gaze locked on Willa's unmoving body. He tripped. Righted himself. And dashed over to her. Dropping to his knees, he pulled her into his lap and felt for a pulse.

She was alive! Her breathing shallow from the drug the killer had used on her, but she was going to be okay.

Chapter Twelve

"You shouldn't have called him," Willa said to Daniel, lying in the bed in the emergency room, holding Zeke's hand.

Daniel gave her one of those sympathetic looks that was starting to grow on her. The inkling of a beard was developing after two days of not shaving and she liked the facial hair on him. Liked it a lot.

"I had to," Daniel said, relief on his sharp features. "He deserved to know what you've just been through."

The last thing she wanted was for her son to know that she had almost been murdered by a serial killer. Unable to ever squash his fears, he'd have nightmares for the rest of his life, always worried whenever she was on duty.

Even though, technically, she hadn't been on duty when that madman attacked her.

"I'm glad he told me, Mom." Zeke stood at her bedside in an oversized sweatshirt and jeans. His dark hair carefully and deliberately mussed.

Taking in both of them at once, with no one fighting or fussing, except for her, they'd never looked so good to Willa.

Tears pricked the corners of her eyes, but she blinked them back, not wanting Zeke or Daniel to see her break down or give them any indication she was unnerved and scared. She had been stalked, attacked and almost murdered. The very idea of the killer knowing where she lived made her blood run cold, and her assailant was still out there, on the loose, most likely planning to terrorize her again.

Luckily, her injuries were minor. Grade 1 whiplash that didn't necessitate a cervical collar. A cut on the side of her head that had required four stitches. A dislocated shoulder, which the doctor had fixed by popping the ball portion back into the socket. It ached right now and would be sore for the next couple of days, but it wasn't anything ice and pain relievers couldn't take care of.

"It's my job to worry about you, not the other way around. Got it?" she said.

But it was too late for that. Her son's skin was paler than usual and the shadows under his eyes were deep. Zeke had been concerned. Scared.

Which made two of them. She glanced at Daniel, her gaze lingering on the lines creasing his brow. Make that three of them.

"Come on, Mom." Zeke rolled his expressive Zach-like eyes. "You and Grandma are the only real family I have. We are supposed to worry about each other."

More tears threatened to well. "Does that mean you're going to be an angel from now on and cause me less stress?" Willa asked, needing to lighten the mood for all their sakes.

Success. She managed to pry a smile out of him. Not a toothy, make your cheeks ache smile, but a real grin.

"Let's not push it by asking for two miracles in one day," Zeke said.

Willa tried and failed not to chuckle, but Daniel laughing, too, reminded her that she needed to do more of that. Not less. "Until you get your heat turned on, I want you to stay with your grandma."

"Why? Do I have to?" Zeke looked as if he had been ordered to seminary school instead of being expected to accompany his grandmother to church once a week. "You're going to be discharged tonight."

She slid her gaze to Daniel in a quiet plea for help. This was a truth her son didn't need to know.

"You're right, Zeke. I am your mom's boy-friend," Daniel said, and Willa's eyes flared wide as her son's jaw dropped a little. "After this incident, I'm going to be around more and she's going to need a lot of extra rest over the next few days."

Zeke nodded. "Yeah, sure."

When her son wasn't looking at her, she mouthed to Daniel, *What are you doing?*

He shrugged.

"Once I'm a hundred percent and I've wrapped up this case, things will go back to normal. Okay?" When he didn't respond, she repeated, "Okay?"

"I got it." He stared at her with eyes that reminded her so much of his father. "But I'm going down to the gas company tomorrow, so it's not a big deal. I just don't want you lying to me if you're in danger or something. I'm grown. I can handle it. You don't have to keep treating me like a child."

Willa's throat closed. "It isn't safe for you to be at my house. Not right now."

"Then it isn't safe for you to be there either."

"I agree," Daniel chimed in.

She did not sign up for them to gang up on her. "I haven't thought through the logistics yet."

"You can stay with me," Daniel offered.

Zeke eyed him. "Or with Grandma. If I had a spare bed in the trailer, you'd be welcome to it."

There was no way she would ever stay with Irene. Under any circumstances. "It isn't safe for me to be with family. I'd only endanger you." That monster could find her simply by watching the police station and the sheriff's department and follow her from there anytime he pleased. And her nightmare wouldn't cease until they had him in custody or he was dead.

Zeke tightened his grip on her hand, and she didn't miss the shadow that crossed Daniel's eyes. "Are you going straight back to work?" her son asked.

"Yeah. There's a bad guy out there and he needs to be stopped before he kills anyone else."

Daniel raised an eyebrow. "There is a sheriff on the case."

"Are you saying you don't need me?"

"No." He shook his head. "I'm not saying that at all," he said, and it was clear to her that he was talking about more than the case. "I am saying that it's fine to rest and recover. You went through…an ordeal."

"You should listen to him, Mom."

This had to stop. Reaching over, she pushed the call button for a nurse, with her IV connection pulling at her wrist. It was time to get out of there. Morning would come before she knew it and she wanted to be ready. "Sitting around, watching TV and twiddling my thumbs isn't going to help me. And it isn't going to help this case get solved any faster either. Physically, I'm fine. Even the doctor said I don't need down time."

Daniel's expression turned somber as he caught what she didn't say. She wasn't fine on other levels that she was not going to touch with a ten-foot pole until they caught the creep who had made the mistake of going after her tonight.

The door opened and a heavyset nurse with rosy cheeks swept in. "Can I get you something?" she asked and hit a button, switching off the call light.

"Yes. I'd like to be released. As soon as possible," Willa said. "The doctor mentioned I wouldn't have to spend the night and I'd rather be on my way."

"I'm not sure if the doctor is ready to discharge you." The nurse frowned. "But I'll go check, Chief."

"Thanks. Appreciate it."

The nurse backed out of the door, and Zeke's lips twitched. "Mom, why do you do this job? I know we need cops to keep people safe and for law and order. But why do *you* do it, knowing the risks, how dangerous it is?"

"You come from a long line of cops. When I was a bit younger than you, I swore I would never become a police officer. I fought it for as long as I could. I was called to do this job. It fits. It's a part of me. It makes me happy."

He looked her over, from head to toe lying in the hospital bed. "You don't look very happy. And I don't mean just now."

Of course, he'd noticed her living half a life. "I'm planning to make changes. I'm going to stop denying myself the things that fill me with joy and have nothing to do with my job." She glanced at Daniel, and she saw the recognition in his eyes. "I know you were happy on the compound," she said to her son. "But I want you to work on being happy out here, too."

Sighing, Zeke lowered his head. "Yeah, I know. It's just been…hard."

She understood better than he realized. "Change is hard. But possible. And it doesn't hurt to have help along the way," she said, giving his hand a long squeeze.

Her son tightened his fingers around hers and squeezed back.

Progress. If nearly dying was the crucial element needed to break the storm between them, she'd do it all over again.

She looked at Daniel. A smile slid from one side of his mouth to the other, and a tingle trickled through her. She couldn't help but wonder if this was the start of something real and wonderful that might actually last.

Then she thought better about tempting fate.

THE NEXT DAY, Daniel tried to act like nothing had changed. But in fact, everything was different.

He had finally acknowledged to himself how deep his feelings ran for Willa. The woman whose beauty and backbone had first caught him off guard. She was smart as a whip, athletic and had a sassy sense of humor that never failed to surprise him.

Willa appeared open to exploring her emotions for him. Not only because she had agreed to stay with him for the time being, but in all her truth sharing with her son, she hadn't disputed that they were dating. Zeke's hostility level had dropped from DEFCON 2, next step to nuclear war, to DEFCON 4, strengthened security measures.

Thought most significant and troubling was that Willa, the chief of police, had gone from being the hunter to being the hunted.

He wasn't going to lie to himself, it had kept

him awake last night while he ensured Willa slept safely at his ranch.

"Let's hear your theory you wanted to run by me last night," he said to her in his office.

Willa looked good, strong and healthy, for a woman who had come close to dying last night. Her shoulder ached and she had taken pain relievers this morning. All in all, her spirits were high. He only hoped she wasn't putting on a brave face because she thought he needed her to. He didn't.

"I was thinking about Zeke's anger during your interview," Willa said, "when he talked about McCoy and how he wanted Marshall to hurt."

"I think there are plenty of folks in town who feel the same way he does. We passed a couple of them on the street celebrating as they read the headlines about his arrest."

"I'm not talking about schadenfreude," she said, referring to pleasure derived by someone from another person's misfortune. "Is there an English equivalent of that?"

"Epicaricacy."

"You just happen to know that?" she asked, and he nodded. "Your mother bought you an excellent education. Money well spent. Anyway, that's not what I'm referring to. McCoy caused pain on a deep level for Zeke when he took away *paradise*. I felt his pain as he talked about it. I believe the killer might be someone who feels like that."

"If it was a copycat, I could see that," Daniel said. "But how do you explain the Holiday Elk Horn Killer stopping five years ago?"

"I think he found the Shining Light. Perhaps to hide out at first. But after a while he started believing. McCoy worked wonders with Zeke. I think it's possible that he might have done the same for the Holiday Killer. Then something happened a couple of months ago and he got kicked out. Now he's angry, bloodthirsty kind of angry, and wants to hurt McCoy and the cult in the process with these new murders. That's why this time he's targeting women with some previous affiliation to the cult."

Taking a sip of his coffee, Daniel leaned forward. "But we've already looked at the Fallen who were sent away this year before Beverly Fisher was murdered."

Nodding, she flashed him a knowing smile. "What if there is another category of people who were robbed of paradise, but aren't the Fallen?"

"It sounds like you're asking me a riddle," he said.

"Exactly. Haven't you felt like if we could crack the code and ask the right question that we would get all our answers from someone in the Shining Light?" she asked.

"Déjà vu. I felt that way yesterday when I was interviewing Marshall. When I started asking him certain questions about the murder case, he actually gave me answers." Yes and no responses. Still, it counted. "Until Huck got him to stop talking."

"We need our very own Shining Light Decoder," she said. "I'd call Mercy, but I don't know if she would be up for it."

Daniel looked out at the bullpen. *Talk about timing.* "Only one way to find out. Why don't you ask her?" he said, pointing to Mercy as she strolled from the front around to his office.

Mercy smiled. "Sheriff Clark. Chief Nelson." She wore blue jeans and a purple sweater.

Even though she was going on over a month of freedom from the compound and their rules, and no longer had to only wear white, to this day it was strange seeing her dressed in other colors.

"What are you doing here?" Willa asked. "I was just talking about you."

"I'm here to see my father. He called me last night and asked me to come visit him. Why were you talking about me?"

"It was nothing bad," Daniel clarified, picking up on the uncertainty in her voice.

"I was saying that we need a Shining Light Decoder because we're not asking the right questions."

Mercy stepped into the office. "I have time to be of assistance this morning. Is there anything I can do to help?"

"Maybe. Are there ever any people who are denied *paradise*, aren't allowed to stay on the compound, but aren't considered the Fallen? Not the transients, who don't care and are only looking for three hot meals and a safe bed. Believers who aren't Starlights."

Mercy sat in the chair beside Willa, facing the desk. "Sure," she said. "It happens, but it's rare."

"What do you mean?" Daniel asked.

"Recruits are usually allowed to stay for as long as they like as adults, no pressure to take vows. While with us, they learn our ways, learn about the Light, are given a function on the compound and trained accordingly."

Daniel took out his pad and reviewed his notes. "Do they still where blue, the color of novices?"

"Not once they've been with us for a year or more," she said, as if the question was silly. "By then, they've become embedded in the community. A part of the commune. The only functions they can't serve in are as leaders and council members. When a person has decided that they're ready to take their vows, they go through their unburdening session with Empy—" she said, stopping herself, "my father and sometimes, and it is rare, he sees too much darkness in a person's heart to allow them to join us. Once that happens, they are cast out, but they aren't labeled, branded like the Fallen."

It had been a riddle, but would solving it uncover a killer?

Daniel exchanged a glance with Willa, her warm brown eyes bright and animated, he could almost feel the buzz of excitement sizzle through her veins as it did his.

Nodding, Willa grabbed the logbook she'd gotten from the garage. "This shows not only who the drivers were, but also the passengers who were dropped off. We've been dismissing the transients, not realizing that some of them, a small, rare group, aren't drifters at all, but people who had built a life on the compound and were ready to commit until Marshall deemed them unworthy and cast them out with nothing. No purpose. No home. No family. Alone and angry. I'm betting one of them is our serial killer." She turned the book toward Mercy. "Do you recognize any names that fit the parameters of who we're looking for?"

"How far back do you want me to go?" she asked.

They'd been looking at the last year, but it didn't hurt to go back a little farther. "Look at everyone over the past two years," Daniel said, handing her a notepad and pen to jot down names.

"Can we get you anything?" Willa asked. "Coffee, tea, soda?"

"A bottle of water?"

Willa was about to get up when Daniel motioned for her to stay seated. Instead of being in the office, she should be home resting. He wasn't going to argue. Not with everything else that was happening. If she was in the office, he could be sure she was safe.

He grabbed Mercy a bottle of water and handed it to her.

Sitting back down, he became exceedingly aware of the clock ticking off the seconds, of Willa's nervous energy as she paced, the tension evident on Mercy's features as she flipped the pages and scanned the names.

Daniel caught up on some paperwork while Mercy reviewed the logbook. He thought he'd have more time to complete a full task and mark it off his to-do list, but he wasn't complaining when Mercy closed the book.

She took a long swallow of water and held out the notepad.

Willa practically snatched it from her grasp and looked down at the list. "Are you sure? Only one name?"

One?

Another long drink of water. "I'm sure," she said, looking confident. "My father has listened to hundreds and hundreds of people unburden themselves. Not all who come to us are good. But we, they, *my father*, knew that the Light was capable of making most individuals worthy through powerful miracles, changing hearts, saving souls of all kinds. Like I said it's a rare occurrence for him to refuse to let someone take vows and join the community."

Willa sat beside Mercy. "How long was he at the compound?"

The young blonde thought about it. "I remember after my father had announced it was my twenty-first birthday, that man approached me and told me that it was too bad I wouldn't get the chance to celebrate it properly in a bar. I found the comment inappropriate and offputting."

"He was there at least four years," Willa said, and Mercy nodded. "Fits our timeline for the Holiday Killer, as well. What section did he work in?"

"Security," Mercy said.

"He had the code to the shed where everyone keeps their belongings from the outside world and could've stolen Zeke's ring," Willa said. "Planted it to throw suspicion away from him."

"What's his name?" Daniel asked. He was going to get every available deputy on the task of tracking down where he lived and worked. Then they were going to bring him in today and put an end to this.

Willa turned the pad to face him.

Simon Yates.

Chapter Thirteen

Willa sat in the passenger seat of the lead vehicle with Daniel behind the wheel. There were two more sheriff's SUVs behind them. None of them had on sirens, but all the vehicles had switched on their flashing lights.

"I can't believe Simon Yates has been under our noses the entire time," she said. "This just goes to show that sometimes the simplest answer is sitting right in front of us."

She wasn't sure if it was a cop thing or just a human thing to complicate things. Like the harder it was to get something gave it more value.

"What I find unbelievable is that he's working as a janitor at the church right across from the bus station. He could sit and watch every single Starlight or drifter being dropped off by the Shining Light van," he said. "From that vantage point, he could also scope out the surveillance cameras of the bus station, to know precisely where to stand so as never to be caught on the security feed."

Yates had failed to take into consideration the surveillance of the convenience store next to the bus station. Cameras covered the store's parking lot and gave a view of the soup kitchen and the church, which showed Yates not only interacting with all three victims, but also him taking Gemma Chavez into the church. She never left through the front or side doors. No surveillance footage was available showing the rear of the house of worship.

Daniel slapped the steering wheel, and she gave him a what-is-it look. "To think, after Simon Yates was kicked out, his first victim was Beverly Fisher, the drug-addicted young woman who had been dropped off at the church."

"Simon had only been out of the compound for a month and working at the church for three weeks. His emotions still must have been raw, like Zeke's now. He probably started thinking about the idea after he saw Beverly. Then for seven months, he lined up his victims, stalked them, learned their routines and habits before killing them. Can you imagine the degree of patience and level of planning that required?" After last night, she could imagine a multitude of horrible things Yates was capable of.

"Gemma Chavez is the exception to how he operated with the others," Daniel said. "Even then, he was able to act quickly, impulsively, decisively without being seen."

Willa shook her head. "He was seen all the time as a janitor. The problem is no one bothered to notice him. That's why he wasn't caught."

"Father O'Neill has no idea he has allowed a murderer to live rent-free in the basement of the church. With a key, he can come and go as he pleased."

They pulled up to the church located across the road from the main bus station that served as a hub for the university's Secure Ride, as well as Greyhound and Amtrak. Daniel parked in front of the church while the remaining deputies covered the other two exits to ensure Simon Yates did not get away and slip through their fingers if he decided to run.

Suspects tended to run for a number of reasons—survival instinct, fear, panic. The worse the crime, the higher the odds.

"Are you good to go on this?" Daniel asked. The worry in his eyes was touching. "There's no shame being part of the backup."

No shame for him. For her, most certainly there was. "Don't try to sideline me or put me on the B team." Willa could handle a dash and chase. The ache in her shoulder wouldn't stop her from running, though tackling a suspect would prove tricky. Not impossible. She'd have to watch her sore shoulder, but the doctor had cleared her for duty.

Daniel had taken steps to mitigate fight or flight of the suspect from occurring with six of them, three teams of two going in through the only entrances: front, rear and east side.

The time of day was ideal. The church was open, and neither mass nor confession was on the schedule now. The soup kitchen next-door would not get started for another two hours.

Once the other two teams radioed in that they were in position, Daniel said, "We're a go."

Weapons drawn, Daniel and Willa entered through the front. They had a visual on Russo and Livingston. Cody and another deputy weren't visible from the far end of the church.

Father O'Neill was sitting in a pew reading scripture. He jumped to his feet, his head on a swivel as he processed the sight of them. "What is the meaning of this?"

"Simon Yates, Father," Daniel said. "Where is he?"

Wild-eyed, O'Neill hesitated. "Are you sure you're looking for the right man? Simon is hardworking and kind. Has he done something wrong? Perhaps it's a misunderstanding."

Shaking her head, Willa wanted to pull Father O'Neill aside and set him straight, but they'd have to explain later.

"Where?" Daniel repeated the single word.

The priest pointed a trembling finger to a door. "In the basement. That's where he stays. Try not to hurt him."

Tell that to the seven women he's savagely killed.

Daniel took point, reaching the door first, and signaled to her with his eyes. Willa put a hand on the knob. Slowly, she checked it, turning the knob ever so slightly. Unlocked. She slid a glance to Daniel.

One curt nod was the signal. She opened the door, revealing a staircase. He cleared it and headed down. Willa was right behind him, and Livingston followed. The other three remained upstairs near the entrances, on the slim chance that Yates got past them, he was not getting out of that church.

In the basement, they entered a wide corridor. Daniel directed Livingston to the left. The deputies opened the two doors at the end of the hall, looked inside the rooms and closed them. Deputy Livingston made a sharp back and forth motion across his throat, letting them know it was a dead end, and mouthed, *Supplies.*

A toilet flushed up ahead to the right. The three of them swiveled, focusing on the precise point of the sound.

Bathroom down the hall.

The door swung open, and Yates stepped into the corridor, carrying a magazine, wearing a sweater, jeans and boots. He was a big guy in his thirties. Tall. Sturdy build.

With weapons trained on him, Daniel said, "Simon Ya—"

The guy dropped the magazine and darted across the hall, disappearing into another room.

They always run.

And it was their job to pursue them no matter what.

The three of them took off after him. At the threshold, she and Daniel each took a position on either side. She peeked around the doorjamb and checked the room. Storage: stacked tables and chairs. A quick glance to the floor.

Clear. Willa swept into the room first. Then Daniel was at her back and Livingston was bringing up the rear.

They hustled through to find another corridor and came to a cozy a space that looked as if he was using it as a makeshift bedroom.

There was a cot, sleeping bag, magazines and toiletries.

The hallway up ahead was dark.

She hated dark rooms since there could always be a nasty surprise waiting—like a suspect hiding in a corner with a loaded gun.

Livingston took point. Moving forward with caution, he ran a hand along the wall. He must've found a switch, and the lights flickered on.

No sign of Yates.

They hustled to the next room. The door was closed. She yanked it open, and it was also pitch-black inside. There was a faint humming noise of machinery, and the temperature was several degrees warmer. She guessed it was a boiler room.

Reaching her hand inside against the wall, she groped for a light switch. Found it and flipped it on. Once again, no Yates, but this was the last room. He was probably hiding inside somewhere.

The three of them exchanged glances. With a nod from her, Daniel crept inside first, and they swept into the room behind him, searching the corners and behind the equipment.

Then she saw it. An opening in the wall behind the boiler. A steel plate the size of a door had been removed. She signaled the others.

Grabbing her flashlight from her duty belt, she clicked it on and shone the light inside.

It was a tunnel.

"What the hell?" she muttered.

Daniel peeked inside and keyed his radio. "Suspect is getting away on foot through what looks like an old bootlegger tunnel that was used during prohibition. Russo find out where this one leads. Cody put out an APB. White. Six-one. Two hundred pounds. Rust-colored hair. Blue eyes. We're in pursuit." He slipped inside.

She and Livingston were right behind him.

Footsteps pounded up ahead in the dark. Yates was making a break for it.

Flashlights up and sidearms at the ready, the three of them bolted down the tunnel. Her adrenaline level was off the chart, determination fueling her, she no longer felt any aches.

DANIEL RAN FULL speed after Yates. Willa was right on his heels, but from the sound of it Livingston lagged a bit behind.

They came to a fork in the tunnel and had to choose. Right or left? Closing his eyes, he listened, trying to hear over the pounding of his heart.

"Right," Willa said, darting past him in that direction.

Just in case she was wrong, he directed Livingston to take the other tunnel because there was no way in hell that he was leaving Willa alone or letting Livingston go with her.

They rushed down the tunnel after Yates. He was navigating in the dark, but he was fast—already familiar with the underground system. He probably had used this network of tunnels to help him orchestrate his crimes.

A sliver of light winked up ahead. Drawing closer, Daniel saw a door as he came to the end of this tunnel. He eased open the door, bracing himself for a sneak attack, or a potshot.

But nothing happened, which meant that Yates was getting away.

They entered another maintenance room. At first, he had no idea where they were. Hurrying through into the next room, they came to a hall. They were in another basement. Based on the signs, they were in the library. On the university campus.

Daniel quickly led Willa up to the main floor and down a corridor that opened to the foyer.

Simon Yates dashed through the front doors outside.

If they didn't hurry, they could lose sight of him and then he might disappear forever. They weaved around the folks in the foyer, making their way to the doors. Outside, they each turned in different directions, scanning the area for him.

"Hey!" a young woman cried as Yates pushed her to the ground.

The tall guy shoved through a gaggle of students, knocking another down as he ran toward the Watson Hall building—a twelve-story residence hall. There were too many students around to take a clean shot. The guy crossed the lawn in great, long strides and stormed into the building.

In hot pursuit, Daniel and Willa were right behind him. He keyed his radio. "SWU campus," he said in between hard, ragged breaths. "Watson Hall."

They shoved through the door, scanning the lobby. Where was he?

Daniel recalled there was an underground tunnel from this building to the dining center to accommodate students in the winter. But then he caught sight of Yates.

In the opposite direction, running past the bank of elevators, the man pushed through the door to the stairwell. They sprinted after him, made it through the door in time to see him racing up the steps past the second floor, shoving kids out of his way, slamming them into the wall. Once again, too many students in the stairwell to risk firing his weapon.

Why couldn't more of them be lazy and take the elevator?

"Out of the way!" Daniel yelled to the kids who stood frozen.

They chased after Yates, ascending floor after floor; the higher they went the more the students thinned out in the stairwell.

His thighs were on fire, muscles burning by the eighth level. If Willa felt the strain of the rapid climb, she didn't show it. The top levels were empty except for the suspect and them. "Police! Stop!" Daniel squeezed off three shots, but the guy kept going. He got back on the radio. "Headed to the roof. Watson Hall."

Up three more flights for Daniel and Willa, almost to the top of the tallest building in town, but the man threw open the door to the roof and slammed it shut behind him. Once they reached it, Daniel eased open the roof door. They were met with a deep silence, nothing but the wind.

There were too many places to hide up there. Housings for the air-conditioning units served as dividers down the length of the roof, and Yates could be behind any of them.

"Let's get him," Willa whispered fiercely.

Nodding, Daniel wanted nothing more than

to collar this guy. Holding himself perfectly still, he listened for any sound, any noise to give Yates away. There. Panting came from fifteen feet away. He indicated where to Willa and she signaled that she was going around the other way. Daniel edged forward, treading light on the rooftop gravel. Ten feet, eight, five, and the man jumped up like a grouse flushed from the brush.

The guy bobbed and weaved, trying not to get pinned down or shot.

Daniel charged and pounced on him, taking him down to the gravel top. They wrestled, twisting, throwing knees and punches, each trying to gain the advantage. Daniel went for the arm he'd injured on the guy last night, but nothing brought him pain. He slammed the guy's head into the metal housing of the air conditioner.

At the same time, Yates threw a fist to his kidney. The pain was shocking, and Daniel lost his grip on him.

They both scrambled up to standing. Stumbled and staggered.

Willa trained her gun on the suspect. "Don't move."

Raising his palms, Yates was close to the edge and moved closer still.

"Not another step!" Willa warned.

"Or what?" Yates asked and spit blood from his mouth.

"Or I will send you straight to hell where you belong," she said, the gun not wavering in her steady grip.

The creep smiled, his teeth bloody. "I'm already in hell. Ever since Marshall cast me out. Want to join me?"

"You tried that last night," Willa said. "Never again."

Confusion contorted his features. "Tried what?"

Regaining his breath and his strength, Daniel snatched his handcuffs from his duty belt. "You can pretend all you want. We know you're the one who attacked her last night, you monster. You've already murdered seven women and you're going to rot in jail for it." He stepped forward to cuff him.

Yates moved back onto the ledge.

What was he doing? Daniel stood still while Willa kept her gun pointed at him.

"You think I killed seven?" A sinister smile spread across Yates's face. "Then I did good and he'd be proud. But I can only claim three," he said.

No, no. Damn it.

There were *two* killers after all.

"He? He who?" Willa asked.

"The hunter," Yates said. "I woke him up. Or maybe you did." He stared at Willa, his gaze raking over her. "Either way, if he came for you last night, he won't stop until he's tasted your blood and stabbed your pretty little heart."

Not if I can help it, Daniel thought with a sudden burst of renewed fury.

This was the Starlight Killer. A copycat of the cold case murderer. Which meant the man—*the hunter*—who came for Willa was hiding, plotting, waiting for another chance to strike.

This wasn't over. Not even close. And it never would be until they found the first killer and stopped him. One way or another for good.

"We can work out some kind of deal," Daniel said, desperate to get Simon to cooperate and give up a name, "with the district attorney for a lighter sentence, if you tell us the name of the hunter. You don't have to face a sentence of life imprisonment." More like three consecutive life sentences. "Just tell us who he is."

Yates eased back, shifting his heels off the ledge, over the side. "Don't worry about finding him. He'll find her. And you're right. I don't have to spend the rest of my life in prison." Extending his arms wide, Simon Yates tipped backward, and fell, disappearing over the edge.

"No!" Willa screamed, reaching for him, but Daniel grabbed her by the shoulders, hauling her back and away from the side. She turned, facing him. "We needed that creep alive! We needed him to tell us so we can end this."

"Yes, if Yates hadn't just killed himself and had told us the truth about the hunter's identity, it would've made this easier. But easy or not, we aren't going to give up. Do you hear me? *I* won't stop until we find that sick bastard," he vowed, meaning every single word.

Chapter Fourteen

In the sheriff's office, Willa didn't know how to rid herself of the anxious energy bubbling inside her. She was still on edge.

On the roof of Watson Hall when Yates had talked about the hunter coming for her, to taste her blood and stab her pretty little heart it had been as if a cold, dark wind had blown straight through her soul, chilling her to the bone.

How dare that guy say such awful things and then take the coward's way out? Did he think she was going to crawl up into a pathetic ball, hide away in her house and wait for a serial killer to come for her?

I woke him up. Or maybe you did, Simon had said.

A chill slithered through her body, but she refused to dwell on it.

She didn't operate that way. Letting her mind wander down a dark, twisted path that suggested monsters prevailed or that she had provoked one wasn't going to happen. It was a slippery slope.

Daniel came back into the office along with Mercy who handed her a piping-hot mug.

Willa took a sip and gagged. It wasn't coffee. "What is this?"

"Tea," Mercy said. "Chamomile with honey."

"It's awful," she said, making a face.

"It will calm you down," Mercy said.

Willa set the mug on the desk. "I don't want to calm down," she snapped. "I want to find the man who ran me off the road and stalked me like I was his prey."

"Lowering both your blood pressure and anxiety is always better," Daniel said, and she opened her mouth to protest. "And before you fight me on this just try it. Drink one cup while we run an idea by you."

Frowning, Willa picked up the mug and took another sip. Second time around it was still awful, but it was only one cup. "What's the idea?"

"On our way back here after Simon Yates committed suicide," he said, "I replayed all our theories about who the killer could be and I believe you and I are both right."

She grimaced through another sip. "But we had different suppositions."

He nodded. "I thought it was someone on the outside who was angry and wanted to retaliate. Our Starlight Killer turned out to be Simon Yates. You believed the killer is someone at the compound, who's been hiding out for years, living off the grid. I think that's exactly what the hunter is doing. It's like you said, it's the perfect cover."

Willa leaned forward with interest. "Today is the deadline for them to provide us with a list of individuals who have been there for years and haven't taken their vows."

"There'll be multiple names," Mercy said. "Ten or more."

The number sounded so big, and depressing, compared to Mercy's earlier list of one.

"Ultimately, where will it get us?" Daniel asked, his words generating new anger in her. "We'll question them and the guilty party will lie and evade. We won't be able to prove anything, and you will still be in danger."

None of this was making her feel any better. Not the tea. Not his prelude to an idea, which she had yet to hear.

"What if I told you there's a way to not only identify the killer," he said, "but to have him in custody today and to get the evidence we need to lock him away for the rest of his life, within less than forty-eight hours?"

Willa didn't even try to hide her skepticism. "I'd ask what's the catch. How could that be possible?"

"Through her," Daniel said, pointing to Mercy.

"Yesterday, the sheriff asked if he could give my father my phone number because he wanted to speak with me," Mercy said. "I've worked hard to move on, and I wasn't sure how I felt about it, so I said no. This morning, he had a legal document sent to me. It would essentially make the compound mine and free to do with it as I please."

"But how?" Willa asked. "You're one of the Fallen, the Starlights aren't allowed to speak with you."

"I don't know what his plan is. That's why he wants to talk to me. Anyway, I kept stalling. But it wasn't until you all came back, and I learned Simon is dead and you're still in danger that I understood why."

Willa crossed her arms. "Not to sound ungrateful, but I'm not getting how these two things are related."

"My father wants something from me. It's important to him. That puts me in a position of power where I can ask for something in return. The identity of the killer who is hiding on the compound. If anyone knows, it's him, and I can get him to talk."

There was no doubt in Willa's mind Marshall was aware of all the secrets that his people were hiding. "We could possibly find out who," she said with a nod. "But how do we get the evidence that will convict him?"

Daniel smiled. "I've worked it out with Mercy."

"This all sounds," Willa said, with a shake of her head, "a little too good to be true."

"Sometimes the simplest answer is sitting right in front of us," he replied. "You told me that earlier in the car. Then it occurred to me what the cleanest solution might be."

"Perhaps so. I'm just not used to simple." Willa sipped her tea. "Mercy, in order for you to ask your father for something, don't you have to agree to whatever he wants?"

"I'm sure I can come up with some conditions of my own," Mercy said, leaning forward and putting a hand on Willa's wrist. "We're talking about a serial killer who has set his sights on you. This is your life."

"This is your life, too." The young woman only recently broke free. Willa didn't want to be the one to take away all her new possibilities in the outside world, not even to bring a killer to justice.

"After talking with the sheriff, I think this plan will work. You can have peace of mind. Tonight," Mercy said. "You deserve that. Everyone does." She patted the back of her hand. "Let's go. He's waiting for me in one of the interview rooms."

Willa was stunned they had been working behind her back, albeit to ensure her safety, and their plan was ready to be executed. Right. Now. Her gaze bounced from Daniel to Mercy. "I don't want you to regret this."

"I won't agree to anything that gives me qualms," Mercy said, gently. "All right?"

Willa nodded "Thank you." But it still felt like they were asking too much from her.

"Putting the Holiday Killer behind bars isn't just for you," Mercy said. "It will make the compound safer. It'll show the town that we value the law more than loyalty, and the families of the cold case victims need closure. It's been far too long."

For someone so young, she was wise beyond her years.

They walked Mercy down to the interrogation room and let her in. Then Willa and Daniel went to the observation room.

"Do you really think she can get him to talk," Willa asked, "when he must expect that we're listening?"

"If anyone can do this, it's Mercy," Daniel said. "The good news is Huck isn't here."

Willa hoped he was right. With Yates gone, they needed another way to find out who had tried to kill her a mere two miles from her home. And fast. Before he had a chance to go after her again.

Mercy sat down across from her father and placed the legal document on the table between them, setting a pen on top.

"Thank you for coming," Marshall said to his daughter.

Nodding, Mercy folded her hands. "I was shocked to hear from you since you consider me to be one of the Fallen and to be honest, I don't understand why you've sent me this document."

He looked past her at the one-way mirror, almost as though he could see Willa and Daniel standing there. "I'm taking the charges against me very seriously. I'm preparing myself for the possibility of a conviction, and I want to ensure my legacy lives on through you."

Willa turned to Daniel. "It's like he said that for our benefit," she said.

"Maybe," Daniel said, lifting a shoulder. "But Marshall doesn't strike me as someone to accept defeat."

"At some point he has to acknowledge the

reality that there are two witnesses willing to testify against him," Willa said, "in addition to the fact that he's actually guilty."

Marshall turned his focus to his daughter. "The compound, the commune of five hundred," he said to Mercy, "the belief in the Light, the core values, can all be maintained with you at the helm, overseeing things in conjunction with the council of elders."

She scoffed. "You branded me one of the Fallen. No one in the commune will look at me or speak to me. They believe I must be shunned."

The same fate, or rather plight, as Zeke. Willa had never considered how much harder the circumstances must be for Mercy since she grew up on the compound.

Marshall reached across the table and covered his daughter's hands with his. "Forgive me. I was angry and hasty and misguided. You did not reject the Light or the commune. You rejected me. Your father. That's the message I've already communicated to Huck and asked him to spread it to everyone in the hopes you agreed to this. You were always meant to lead. I was just too tainted to see it."

Mercy expelled a heavy breath. "I have a new life now."

Nodding, he leaned back in his chair. "I'm aware. How is Rocco?" her father asked.

"He's good. We're happy together and with the way things are. The council of elders doesn't need me to run things. They can do it by themselves."

Willa glanced at Daniel. "Is she trying to talk him out of this?"

"I don't think so. Sounds like she's asking him to define her value and what she brings to the table," Daniel said.

A sad smile tugged at Marshall's mouth. "Your vision is unique. You can help the Shining Light evolve beyond what it is now. I only ask that you don't let my name be forgotten. I see you capable of building a bridge between the community of this town and the one on the compound, where there won't be protesters at our gate."

"I'm glad you mention it," Mercy said. "With the protesters, their numbers and their anger continue to grow. For me to consider your proposal, I'll need something significant from you."

Marshall hesitated, his brow creasing. "I don't have much to offer from behind bars, but whatever is within my power to give you, I will."

"I hope you mean that. Simon Yates is dead,"

she said, straightening. "Before he took his own life, he admitted that he isn't responsible for trying to kill Chief Nelson last night." Mercy paused, letting that sink in. "He said—the hunter—will go after her again. The same hunter who murdered four women five years ago."

"My dear," Marshall said, lifting a hand to caress her cheek, "if you take over as leader of the compound, you will have access to all the recorded unburdening sessions and will be able to find him yourself."

She moved away from his touch. "Stop. Lying. I don't believe *the hunter* is a Starlight and I don't believe he has an unburdening tape for me to find." Shoving her chair back with a scrape against the floor, Mercy stood. "If you want to play games, then this discussion is over."

Willa was impressed. Mercy was a tougher negotiator than she had expected.

"Wait. Please, sit." Marshall gestured for her to take her seat, and she did. "You're right," her father admitted. "He isn't a Starlight. He and Simon arrived around the same time. Simon was lost, troubled, looking for a place to belong, but the other one seemed like he was running or trying to hide, but many come to us looking to escape something. They became close friends quickly. They bonded over their difficult relationships with their mothers. Based on the things Simon eventually confessed during his unburdening, looking back on it, I believe his friend, who he referred to as the *hunter*, shared details with Simon about the murders he had committed before coming to the Shining Light. The violent things Simon learned from the *hunter* made him fantasize about doing the same thing. Made him hunger to experience the sick thrill. Simon admitted that he looked up to him, admired him, wanted to become the *hunter*. He had even imagined killing some of our members. That's why, after I made him leave, he emulated the hunter's killings, except with Starlights."

"When did you suspect there was such darkness in them?" Mercy asked.

"What makes you think I did before Simon's unburdening?"

Mercy leaned back, disgust twisting her features. "Because I know you, Father. The way you read people, see inside them is remarkable. Please. I need you to be honest with me, or instead of leading the Shining Light, I'll destroy it."

With a sigh, Marshall lowered his head. "I had suspected for quite some time," he said. "I monitored them closely. Neither of them ever laid a finger on anyone in our community,"

Marshall said, as though that somehow made who and what those men were okay. "I found out for certain when Simon chose to unburden in order to ascend and become a member. There was simply too much darkness. The way he fantasized about killing people in our community, I could not make him a permanent member. So I cast him out."

Mercy grimaced. "What about the other murderer?"

"After I made Simon leave, the *hunter* will never unburden out of fear he will be cast out as well."

"How can you let him stay?" she asked, and Willa wondered the same.

There were women and children of all ages on the compound. Surely, Marshall viewed the man as a threat to his community.

"I would never kick someone out based on a suspicion," Marshall said. "A confession is a different matter."

"If you've known all this time who is responsible," Mercy said, "why didn't you tell Chief Nelson and Sheriff Clark?"

Willa could take a guess as to why Empyrean would stay quiet.

"It would reflect poorly on us," he said.

What he really meant was that it would reflect poorly on him.

"The commune would have questioned the sanctity of the unburdening sessions if I had revealed information from one to the police," Marshall said, and Willa was sickened by how he had violated it anyway by blackmailing former members. "And I could visualize the headlines in the *Gazette*: Marshall McCoy unleashes one murderer while harboring another. The Shining Light would not have survived such scrutiny."

"More like Marshall McCoy wouldn't have survived the scrutiny," Daniel said.

It was just as Willa had thought. McCoy was protecting his image above all else, even at the expense of more lives lost. "If he had only told me the truth after Beverly Fisher, I might have been able to save Leslie and Gemma."

"He's despicable," Daniel said. "It makes me wonder what other monsters are hiding on the compound."

Willa nodded. "That's probably another concern he had. The entire town will wonder the same thing."

"Who is he?" Mercy demanded. "Who is the *hunter*?"

Marshall shoved the contract toward her. "Will you help lead?"

"You should know I'll make sweeping changes," Mercy said. "For starters, I won't live in Light House or on the compound and won't require anyone else to either. Rocco and I are happy on his ranch. Also, I think it's time to do away with the color system. We should wear what we want. And I'll welcome back any Fallen member who desires to be a part of our community once more."

Willa wasn't going to jump for joy about that last part. She had just gotten her son back and wasn't ready to lose him again, but Zeke had to make choices for himself.

"I don't fully agree." Marshall shook his head vehemently. "I believe the chaos it'll breed could overwhelm you. But my opinion won't matter. You run it as you like."

Mercy picked up the pen and turned to the last page. "Give me a name. And I'll ensure the Shining Light survives."

"Orion Vansant."

"Ry?" Mercy asked. "From the security team who works in the garage?"

Oh, my God. Willa's gut twisted.

"Isn't he the guard who assisted you in getting Miguel for questioning?" Daniel asked.

"Yes," Willa said, "he was." Admitting it aloud made her skin crawl.

She had spoken with Ry, touched him, ridden on the back of his motorbike. Had she done something to encourage his homicidal attention? She wondered when the hunter had decided to target her. After her first press release or visit to the compound? Or had it been their personal interaction? Putting him up close with a woman who fit the profile of his victims?

Don't go there.

Ultimately, it didn't matter. There was nothing she could've done differently to prevent him from hunting her because every action she had taken had been to do her job.

"Are you all right?" Daniel asked her.

No, no, she wasn't. Not yet.

"I will be," she said. Once she saw the look on Orion's face when they slapped the cuffs on him, and she read him his rights that would go a long way to making her feel much better.

While they waited for the arrest warrant to come in, Mercy contacted Huck at the compound and arranged to have extra security guards posted in and around the garage where Orion was working, oblivious this would be his last day. No one wanted a repeat of what happened with Yates slipping away.

On their approach to the compound, they had foregone the flashing lights and sirens, not wanting to give Ry the slightest heads-up that he was finally going to pay for his crimes.

Willa needed the sense of agency that came

with driving. She sat behind the wheel as they took two sheriff's SUVs to the compound.

Marshall McCoy's message about Mercy had spread like wildfire. Once the guard at the gate had seen her, he had waved them right through. At least a hundred people had gathered on the front lawn of Light House, waiting for her. Not only was she embraced when they arrived, no longer shunned, she was treated like royalty. A large group surrounded her while others waited to talk to her and touch her, their affection for her so genuine.

Willa got of the vehicle with a sense of purpose. Holding the logbook, she headed to the garage with Daniel on one side of her and Livingston on the other.

"Hey, there," Orion said with a bright smile, having the audacity to meet her eyes as they entered the garage. "If it isn't the lovely Chief Nelson, the industrious Sheriff Clark and his trusted deputy. What can I do for you?"

Shawn and two other security guards were tinkering around in the building. From the corner of her eye, she saw them monitoring the situation.

Pulling on her I'm-going-to-enjoy-this smile, Willa said, "Today is about what I have for you." She handed him the logbook.

"All done with it?" Orion asked. "Did you get what you needed from it?"

"Yeah, I think so." Her stomach soured as she considered how he must've thought he had her and the rest of them fooled. *Lovely Chief Nelson. Industrious Sheriff Clark.* Not only was her compliment sexist for focusing on her appearance and the sherifff's work ethic, but he was cocky enough to say it to her face after hunting her like an animal just last night. "Hey, Ry, I've got one more thing for you." As she pulled the warrant from her pocket and handed it to him, the guards closed in around him from the rear.

"What is this?" he asked with a frown, opening it and glancing at the paperwork.

The security guards stopped what they were doing and came closer, taking their cues from Shawn.

"Orion Vansant, you're under arrest," Willa said, drawing the sweetest satisfaction from saying the words.

In nanoseconds, Ry changed, like a switch had been flipped, and he lunged at her, going for her throat, his green eyes bulging with fury. Daniel and another deputy snatched his arms, holding him back, before he had a chance to touch her.

"As I was saying. You are charged with the

murders of Tiffany Cummings, Rose Rossini, Jessica McIntosh, Carla Larsen and with the attempted murder of a police officer, leaving the scene of a crime and obstruction of justice. You have the right to remain silent."

She finished reading him his rights while Daniel handcuffed him. Holding Orion's wrists with one hand, Daniel grabbed his left arm with the other. She watched him apply pressure to the area where Daniel had shot and wounded him last night, and the man winced.

"I don't know what's going on." Ry's face flushed red. "This is a load of crap. Some mistake. You've got this all wrong. I haven't done anything wrong."

Once they reached the sheriff's SUV, Daniel put Orion in the back seat and slammed the door shut. "How do you feel now?" he asked.

"Never better," she said with a wink at him.

Huck cut through the crowd surrounding Mercy and greeted them. "Sheriff. Chief." He held up a disposable bag with a cup. "Inside is Orion's cup from our last meal. That should be all the evidence you need for a conviction."

They already had his DNA from the bite marks on the bodies. Once it matched the DNA from the cup that would be all District Attorney Jennings would need.

Willa glanced over her shoulder at Orion,

the hunter, in the back seat. She breathed a sigh of relief that the monster was going to spend the rest of his life behind bars where he belonged.

"What's on your mind?" Daniel asked her.

"How good it will be that the four families from the cold cases will finally get the closure and justice they deserve."

"Thanks to you," he said with a grin.

She returned his smile. "Thanks to us."

"You have to admit we make a pretty good team, don't we?"

Professionally and personally. She cupped his face—right there in public, for anybody to see—her heart lighter than it had been in weeks. Maybe ever. "Yeah, the best."

Epilogue

In less than forty-eight hours, they'd gotten a DNA match for Orion Vansant and the district attorney had charged him with four counts of first-degree murder among other things. On the Shining Light compound, Mercy and the security team found a hole that had been dug under the fence and hidden with bushes. They believed that was how Orion Vansant was able to get out of the compound without being seen. Daniel's deputies located a car Vansant had been storing at a nearby dude ranch. Under the church in the tunnels Simon Yates had used, they found evidence that he had kept Gemma Chavez down there before killing her. Marshall McCoy pled not guilty to blackmail and was planning to fight the charges.

In the days that followed, Mercy had started implementing her sweeping changes on the compound. One of the most significant was starting family day, where members were encouraged to invite friends and family from the outside to spend the day on the compound together.

Rather than leaping at the chance to rejoin the Shining Light, Zeke had decided to give it a year on the outside. He and Thomas were now roommates, and he no longer had a problem paying his bills.

One month later, standing outside by their vehicles, Daniel held Willa in his arms and looked down into her lovely face. "You've got nothing to worry about."

"Easy for you to say. You're not the one hauling a resistant son into family therapy," she said.

Daniel smiled, holding back a chuckle. "Zeke agreed to go, albeit reluctantly."

"After months of prodding him," she said, sounding exasperated.

"I still call that progress. Also, I've heard that Dr. Delgado is fantastic at what she does. She even helped the FBI with that hostage crisis situation earlier this year."

"Then she's just what we need, considering Zeke is acting like I'm holding him hostage by taking him." Willa frowned, looking overwhelmed.

She only needed to take it in baby steps, one session at a time.

"Trust in the process. Trust in her reputation." He rubbed her lower back, wanting to caress her curves, but drew on his self-restraint. "Most importantly, trust in the bond you and Zeke have. You'll get through this."

The corner of her mouth hitched in a grin as she held him tighter. "How do you always know what I need to hear to feel better?"

He shrugged. "Call it intuition." The truth of the matter was they fit together. A perfect match. He loved her fiery spirit and she loved his grounding calm. It also helped that they understood the pressures, the long hours, the danger they both faced professionally.

"Thanks for not giving up on me. On the possibility of an us."

"You can thank me later." He lowered his head, brushing his lips over hers before taking her mouth in a kiss that showed her precisely how much he wanted her.

"Ugh," Zeke said, coming out of the cabin. "Save it for the bedroom." He got into Willa's car and slammed the door.

Laughing, they pulled apart.

Willa looked at her watch. "You better hurry up. You don't want to be late picking up your mom from the airport."

No, he did not. Selene Beauvais could be late and leave others waiting, but never the other way around. "I should be good. I checked the traffic. The roads to Denver are clear."

Willa climbed into her SUV, started it and rolled down the window. "I can't wait to meet her."

That's what she said now.

"It'll be nice," Willa continued, "having the focus on Grace and Holden and not us. No pressure."

"That's true. No pressure is always my preference." He leaned down, putting his arm on the door. "Thanks for agreeing to come to the family dinner with me."

"Thanks for inviting Zeke." She glanced over at her son, who nodded while on his phone. "He's always been curious what it's like on the Shooting Star Ranch."

"Which reminds me. I mentioned to Holden that Zeke wasn't happy working as a gas station attendant and was hoping to get a position as a ranch hand. He said they're always looking for hard workers who don't mind starting at the bottom. I hope I didn't overstep by throwing your name out there."

"Are you kidding?" His eyes lit up with excitement. "You didn't overstep. That's great. I guess it's not so bad you're my mom's boyfriend."

Daniel laughed. "I guess not."

Willa swatted her son's arm playfully. "Stop it, Zeke." She looked over at Daniel. "Thank you. That was nice of you. You didn't have to do that. We appreciate it."

"Play your cards right, young man," Daniel said, "and you'll even get a tour tonight."

Zeke fist pumped the air. "Yeah."

Wearing a beautiful, bright smile, Willa shook her head.

"See, it's going to be fine. All you have to do is trust me."

"If that's all, then no problem. Because I do trust you. And love you."

"I love you, too." He never got tired of hearing her say the L-word. Leaning closer, he brushed his lips across hers and kissed her slow and soft.

"Ugh," Zeke said. "Save it for later."

"Sure. We'll save it."

"Hey, I've been meaning to throw this out there," she said. "What do you think about us living together?"

Zeke looked up from his phone. "I think it's a brilliant idea. Where would you live? Wayward Bluffs or Laramie?"

Willa smiled. "I was thinking on Daniel's ranch closer to Laramie. Shorter commute."

"Is there a spare room for me when I visit if I wanted to stay the night?" Zeke asked.

"I've got two," Daniel said, and her son made a sound of approval. He did love her and would do everything he could to make things easier, better, for her and Zeke. "We should do it before Thanksgiving."

"Sounds perfect," she said with a nod, and it warmed his heart to see the confidence gleaming in her eyes. "We're going to be fine." She pressed a hand to his cheek and caressed his face. "The three of us."

He was counting on it. "Better than fine."

* * * * *